He Saved Her

Harriet Morgan

Contents

Chapter One

B efore we start:

   I hope that it looks good!!!

□•□•□□•□•

Aurora

The day my sister left for college is the day I finally realized how much pain she was in. How much she endured. How much she had to fight the will to live.

It is also coincidentally the day I also got to experience what she had previously. Of course, I had experienced a small part of it, but from that day everything multiplied faster than germs.

I love my sister, and I love that she is now safe but it does make me sad knowing she is never coming back; leaving me here with a monster I'd have to fend off by myself.

I roll off to my side as I count the amount of steps being taken downstairs. Only 10 more and he will be gone. My thoughts are preoccupied with awaiting for the steps when my phone timer rings letting me know I have five more minutes before I'd have to go to school. Heaving a sigh, I get out of bed and do my routine as quietly as I can. After 4 minutes later, and hushed breaths, I make my way downstairs being careful to not make any sound.

Closing my eyes, I make a beeline for the door, and a small smile plays on my face as I feel the doorknob on my palm. The smile is replaced with a groan when a hand claws at my hair and pulls me backward so abruptly I almost fall. I look back to meet a pair of piercing green eyes and curse myself. He is dressed in a button down and well pressed slacks.

"I didn't-"

"Shut up", he says his voice booming and within a second his hand is met with my cheek. I blink away the tears threatening on the back of my eye, I won't let him have the satisfaction of seeing me weak. Instead, I meet the eyes of the person who gave me the exact same pair and tell myself only 140 more days. I got this, I can do this.

"You forgot to make me breakfast today", he shouts at me and I back away to the door. He laughs at the sight of my fear,"Just leave."

Don't have to be told twice!

I turn around slowly and open the doorknob. I make it out of the house but not before his hand grazes my butt. I bite my lips against the disgust but keep walking off the porch and to a place where I can get a little bit of freedom.

□•□□•□•□•

I sprained my ankle trying to get out of the last classroom in hope to get a head start and make it home before he did. It would give me a good fifteen minutes to make him a late lunch and then head upstairs to hide in the one room where I have safety. But upon rushing out of my last class, I walked too hurriedly and managed to step the wrong way. I had hissed in pain as I stepped off to the side to avoid being trampled.

After a few deep breaths, I had gathered the courage to start walking again. Only when I did my legs buckled in an almost embarrassed way before I sighed and turned to the closest room to me, which was fortunately the nurses room.

"What do we have here?"Her voice scared me as I placed a hand on my heart and stumbled to a nearby chair.

"My ankle", I had wheezed pointing at it and she gave me a sympathetic look. It made me duck my head and instead focus on my breathing. She walked further into her office and came back with a ice pack which she handed to me.

"Just a sprained right?", she asked and I nodded. I put the ice pack on my swollen ankle and hissed in pain.

"Probably not best to walk with it", she said softly, making me look up at her wide brown eyes that cast her oval face together.

"That's my only plan", I whisper, trying not to sound too desperate. "God, it's hot", I add when I realized my breathing had yet to slow.

"You should wait an hour or so. Go wait outside, I heard there's a small practice going on that could distract you", she says making her way to me and placing a hand on my shoulder. I stand up and her hand goes under my arm when I almost fall back down again. She smiles kindly and leads me out of the office and toward the back of the school. When I get there, I try to have her drop me off but she insists on walking me to the bleachers.

"Thank you", I say my voice sounding more sincere than I was going for. She only smiles and says,"I'll see you later, Aurora."

"Bye", my voice is a whisper as she has already started walking off. Sure enough, there is a basketball game going on, but my mind drifts to the semi-good book on my phone and I grab for it. After getting through a few chapters, I hear someone shuffling from behind me.

My throat closed up and my heart starts beating fast. I was the only one here, so the sudden movement made my fists ball up. When I look back, the guy puts his hands up in surrender and stays there. I blink a few times and make out the small smile on his face. My eyes follow his messy wavy hair and hazel thin eyes with eyelashes that make me envy him. His long straight nose fits his face perfectly if not helping him. His cheekbones are hollow, carving out the shape.

"Hi", I blink again realizing he is speaking. I look around and don't find anyone there so I turn back to him and attempt a small smile, which turns up to be more of a grimace. My heart is still beating fast at the uncertainty of this exchange. Furthermore, a guy had never come up to me to talk, which I appreciated.

I didn't appreciate the way his eyes twinkled in a little happiness and the way his lips were always lifted up. "My name is Oliver", he says and my mind flashes to the conversations people have around the school. His name is a big thing in this school as basketball is the biggest sport around here. I haven't seen him this close up until now though and I find that maybe girls were not extragratting on his looks.

"What's your name", he asks softly when I don't respond to his introduction. I open my mouth to answer but my name is stuck in my throat. How long has it been since I've said my own name? My mind flashes to the way my father said my name this morning, how his lips curled up in a disgusted look.

"Aurora", I say despite my heart going 80 miles an hour in my chest. He throws one of legs around and it lands on my row of the stadium. My heart beat picks up and I can feel the hairs on the back of my neck rising. Why is he moving closer to me?

He looks up at me with a widened eye after he has settled down next to me. I look beside me to see my phone extending out to his face. He puts his hands up in the air in front of him again and says,"Sorry, your voice is just so soft, I couldn't hear."

I retract my phone and bring my hands together in my lap. I look down at my hands and say my name again even though the memories of it being shouted at me runs through my head.

I hear a hum and move my head up to meet his eye. "That's a pretty name."

To be shouted in disgust.

I turn away from his gaze and instead focus on the beat up shoes I'm wearing, I should get new ones before people start thinking poorly about me. The white of the shoe has turned into a mess of gray and brown from all the walking I've done since last year. I pick at my nails and look up at him.

"Are you waiting for something?", I ask trying to raise my voice but to no avail. It comes up more of a whisper and I curse myself for not being stronger. His face contorts in confusion before it relaxes in understanding of what I just asked.

"I just", he stops, runs a hand through his hair and runs a tongue over his bottom lip. "I told the guys that you were my girlfriend."

Chapter Two

A urora

My first thought is: what the heck? Then my mind unravels and a whole book of questions pop in my mind the boldest being Why is he talking to me?

Confusion written all over my face, I say,"What?"

He repeats his previous statement again making me release an impatient breath. Does he think I didn't hear him the first time?

"Why?", I ask in a whisper and attempt to look at him. His hair has started to curl at the ends at the sweat in his hair from playing basketball. He shakes his head, his ears reddening at the tip.

"It was...", he stops looks at me and then says,"They kept pressing the situation and I saw that you were the only one in the bleacher so I kind of said it was you."

I grab for my phone and pick up my backpack off the floor by my feet and stand up. "I'm not sure what I should say, but I need to leave", I say not looking at him and attempting to climb down the stadium. I trip on a stair and fall down and feel him move toward me.

"Don't", I say stopping him before he can put a hand on me. I look back and he pockets the hand he had extended toward me. I feel dizzy, I should go I think. I get off the floor and make it down the stadium.

"Are you okay?", he asks confusion written in his voice. I ignore him and walk ahead before having to stop and catch my breath against the brick of the school. Why did I come all the way back here? I can't walk anymore.

"Are you driving home?", he asks and I try to ignore the sound of his voice. My mind is whirling and my thoughts are scattered. One thing for sure is that my foot hurts so bad I feel I'm going to start crying. Blowing out a breath my mind repeats a mantra: You're Strong.

I get off the wall and attempt to walk again only to stop by the wall again. I blow out a raspberry and turn to the guy, my face sweating. "Why are you still here?"

"You need to take pain medicine", he says ignoring my question.

"I need to get home", I say , trying to get my voice higher in an attempt to not feel so weak.

"Are you walking home?", He asks and I nod slowly. He makes a sound of disapproval and then says,"Hand me your backpack, it's weighing you down, and then hop, I'll help you." He reaches out a hand toward me and I stagger away.

"Don't touch me", I say closing my eye and feeling the rush of fear pass through me again. I open my eye to find him a step away from me and instead looking at me with soft eyes.

"Just hand me your backpack then", he says and I take it off and drop it at his feet. He picks it up with two fingers and swings it over his shoulder like it had weighed nothing. "Come on, we'll walk to my car." He starts walking and I hop toward him trying to not look stupid.

"I can walk home", I say as we head into the parking lot. He turns to me and shakes his head,"I'll drop you."

"I don't...", I trail off having wanted to say, I don't feel comfortable around you, but instead say,"I don't know you."

"I'll drop you off, I promise. I wo–"

"Don't even attempt to touch me okay?", I say softly my voice breaking as we make it toward the cars. I hear voices from ahead of us and a loud voice calls out,"Oli."

I look to my right as the guy waves a hand toward his friend and his friend laughs. "Is that your girl?"

"It's uh", he stutters and then nods,"Yeah."

"What's her name?", his friend asks walking toward me and I feel the need to hide. It was bad enough Oliver towering over me but another one? I take a step back but the new guy doesn't seem to notice as he approaches us.

"Aurora", Oliver answers with a soft smile and I tell myself that I should replace the other memories of this one. But the thought escapes as soon as I see my father shouting at me in my head again. "Rory", he says too and I tune back into the conversation.

"Well", the guy turns toward me and extends a hand toward me,"I'm Austin." I freeze and blink a few times but the hand remains. I try to claw my hand away from my sides but it doesn't move, it doesn't want to move.

Oliver glances down at me, sees the panic on my face and down to my fidgeting hand and then turns to his friend.

"Austin, I think Rory would like to go home. She sprained her ankle earlier and had been delayed due to our practice so it's been killing her. Right, babe?", he says glancing at me. My mind blanks at his words but I manage to nod and Oliver waves goodbye to his friend.

"I'm really nice, I promise", the friend shouts to me as he leaves. I look at Oliver but he only laughs at his friend and says,"See you later, man."

"Bye Rory", Austin shouts heading to his car and I try to calm my racing heart. Without saying a word to me, Oliver walks ahead to his car and opens the passenger side door. I stare at the deep green jeep as he places my backpack on the floor and then steps back waiting for me to get in. I continue staring at it and he pulls down something that gives me a lift. Clearing his throat, he says,"Get in."

"And you promise–", I start before he cuts me off.

"I heard you before Austin spotted us, I won't touch you."

"You pr–"

"I promise, Aurora", he says and my heart hurts at the name.

"Call me Rory", I say getting in the car and he nods before closing the door behind me. I pull down the seatbelt over my chest and then pick at my nail. Oliver gets in the car and starts the engine. He glances toward me and places his phone on the dashboard in front of me. "Put your address in there", he says softly.

I pick up his phone, noticing how much nicer it is than my old phone I keep for emergencies and books and type in my address. I place the phone back on the dashboard and he takes it back. He turns on GPS and drives toward my house silently. When he reaches my street, I find my voice and ask,"Why did you call me your girlfriend again?"

Oliver stops at a red light and turns to me, his lips in a frown so different than the last twenty minutes I've known him. "I made a mistake."

I wait for him to go on and he sighs,"I dragged you into this mess. If we broke up today that would be unrealistic as I just told my friends today but I also don't want you playing along to something you don't want."

"Oliver, you know I can't be your girlfriend", I say avoiding looking at him and instead playing with the sleeves of my sweatshirt.

"It would be fake", he says and I frown.

"But there are so many things wrong with this. First, I will not let you touch me so how are people going to believe this. And second, I'm not...well", I say stopping abruptly.

"You're not what, Rory?", he asks and the light turns green fortunately so he doesn't look at me anymore.

"I'm not", I take a deep breath,"Your type."

"How so?", he says.

"I'm, well, I'm me. I don't talk to anyone whereas you are a student athlete so you know everyone adores you", I say heat rising to my cheek at the expense of talking so much. He glances at me for a second before turning back to the road.

"I need someone like you though. Someone who is unexpected for me and so girls will back off me."

"Girls are attacking you?", I ask in a soft whisper and he nods.

"Partly the reason I've been telling them I have a girlfriend. They have been pestering me about it so I gave in and said it was you on the court today."

"And you chose me because I was the first person I saw?", I ask.

"Yes and no", he starts,"Yes and also because you were at the practice so it was easy to pick you. Girlfriends support their boyfriend."

"But nobody is going to believe it", I say.

"They will. I'll tell them this is a lowkey relationship and that we don't do any PDA."

"It's just", I say and slump back in my seat, stopping.

"What is it?"

"I'm not your type of pretty", I say heat rising to my cheeks at my words. He glances at me for a second and I watch as a slow smile takes over his face. My heart beats fast at his smile, it was caused by me. I avert my gaze and look down at my lap nervous.

"You are pretty", he says and I start to open my mouth to object but he continues. "You are. And what do you mean my type of pretty?"

"Well you're pretty", I say and then close my mouth,"I mean, well you know what I mean. And I'm not..."

Oliver chuckles at my rambling and I take notice of the dimples he has, so prominent that it's a surprise it's not there when he isn't smiling. "Rory, you are. You are my type of pretty but more."

"You're just saying that", I say trying to calm my racing heart. The first time a guy has ever called me pretty.

"Trust me. I didn't just pick you out because you were the only option. I picked you because you were pretty", he says and I feel my head buzz with sudden excitement.

"But, Oliver you know that...", I trail off hugging myself.

"I won't touch you", he says pulling into my driveway.

"So how are we going to pull it off?", I say picking up my backpack and avoiding his gaze.

"We'll see tomorrow after I pick you up. Now, don't worry too much about it,but do figure out what you want out of this", he says and I nod.

"Thank you, Oliver. And uh also for the compliment", I say getting out of his car. I wait for his reply before shutting the door.

"Happy to do it, Rory. When should I pick you up?"

"7?", I ask and he nods. I close the door and walk toward my house. On the outside it seems that my dad is not home, but I know that he is and seeing how late I am, I am scared to go. So, I turn to him one more time and say,"Thank you."

"Don't mention it", and then he drives off and leaves me to face my own consequences.

Chapter Three

O liver

I haven't gotten the best sleep after my impulse decision to ask a complete stranger to play my girlfriend. Word got out quick and soon enough people were talking about it online. Most of the guys were congratulating me on finding such a pretty girl, it infrutiated me seeing as nobody knew who she was before this. It dawns on me that I didn't know who she was either. Some of the girls congratulated me while others left not so nice comments.

I spent half an hour reporting all the mean comments about her and afterwards I felt guilty bringing her into this. As she said yesterday, she is not the type of girl to be in public. As I get ready for the day, I try to think of ways to make her feel comfortable around me. First, I make sure I smell good and that I dress nicely as opposed to the sweaty gym set yesterday.

I arrive in front of her house at 7 on the dot and wait for her to come out. Not knowing how her neighbors will respond, I decide against honking. She comes out three minutes later looking more self conscious than she did when I dropped her off. Her backpack is perched on one shoulder on the opposite side of her sprained leg. The thing I'm most worried about is the frown that is settled into her mouth and how she is rapidly blinking. The clothes she is wearing today drowns her more than it did yesterday.

"Are you okay?", I ask her as soon as she gets in, but she only buckles her seatbelt and looks out the window. I ask her the question again and this time she turns to me with a jerk of her head and I take notice of the tear slipping down her eye. My hand aches to remove it but she only says,"Drive."

"Are-"

"Drive, Oliver", she asks louder. This is the loudest I've heard her speak and yet it is not any louder than how I usually speak. Frowning, I pull out of her driveway and start driving to school in utter silence. The whole way I was worried about her but when I park, she turns to me with a small smile and the tears are gone. I blink at how fast her demeanor changed. She only gives me a look and then opens the door to my car and gets out. I get out of the car too and jog to her side and hold out my hand,"Bag."

She hands me the backpack this time rather than throwing it at my feet and then takes a huge step back from me. I frown but we start walking toward the building. Once we get in, all eyes are on us and I stop walking to let Aurora catch up to me. Once she does, I walk slower and hope that people don't ask anything about my new girlfriend walking a good 5 feet away from me. I glance at the way Aurora is looking into the crowd and she hugs her body with her arms.

"Rory?"

"Yeah?", she asks looking up at me and I take a step closer to her. "Can you, I don't know, maybe grab my shirt sleeve. I won't reciprocate that, I promise."

She looks up at me and her lips purse up in thinking. I have the sudden urge to move away the hair that is blocking my view of her face but resist as

I remember the way she had me promise to not touch her. She nods slowly and then takes a step closer to me and her hand makes it's way to the sleeve of my shirt. She fists it up and I grimace at the way this doesn't look like a couple scene but take the win anyways.

"What's your first class?", I ask her and sensing that people are listening I add,"Babe?"

"English Lit 3", she says in a whisper and I nod as we walk toward it. Once we get to her classroom door, I hand her the strap of her bag, making sure to not touch her, and say,"I'll see you at lunch."

"Okay", she asks looking uncertain but I only nod at her encouragely. The people around me start whispering so I call Aurora back and say,"I'll miss you." And then I give her my cheekiest smile and walk away. Right before though, I notice the blush appearing on her skin.

□□•□•□•□•

"Man, are you excited for the game this Friday?", Austin asks as we walk into the lunchroom. I nod and my eyes search for Aurora and I find her waiting at the closest table to the door and I smile at her. She looks out of place so I stop by her and say,"We will eat in the back." I grab her backpack off the floor and she stands up walking by me but not any closer than how Austin is. He looks at me and then toward the girl beside me and he smiles.

"Rory, how are you?", he asks not knowing that she barely talks to me as it is.

"I'm good", she whispers and steps closer to me and grabs my shirt sleeve, stretching it out so she isn't touching me. Austin smirks at me and whispers,"Does she not talk?"

"She is shy", I answered back and he chuckles. I hit him on the shoulder for being an ass but he only laughs.

"She only likes you", he says and my heart stops for a second. I glance at Aurora who is clawing at my shirtsleeve trying to keep up while looking at the floor.

"She is my girlfriend", I shrug and we make it to our table. Aurora lets go of my shirtsleeve and I drop her backpack on the table and the guys and I head to the lunch line. I look back at Aurora who doesn't make an effort to walk with us while instead looking at her phone. I frown but make my way to the lunch line.

After I come back to the table, I have double of everything I'd usually eat. I sit by Aurora and she slides closer to me when she sees Austin sliding in next to her. It's packed here and her eyes are frantic as she tries to separate from us. Is she scared of us? I study her for a minute before whispering,"You're safe here."

"It's just", she starts and then moves closer to me, but not before dropping her backpack in between us. Now her backpack is digging into my torso but I only give her an encouraging smile. I pick off one of the salads off my plate and push it in front of her. She glances at me and then at the food before her eyes flash with panic and she shakes her head.

"Eat", I whisper trying to be encouraging but she shakes her head. I push it closer toward her and say,"Rory, come on." Her face pales but she opens it up and I watch as she plays with the fork the whole lunch period. Toward the end, the group gets loud and Austin finds his way toward Aurora and he accidently body slams into her.

I watch as she jumps up in panic and her face pales even more. "Stay", I whisper to her softly before reaching around her and pushing Austin off of her. He glances at me with a smile and then at Aurora who looks close to tears. My heart aches for her and I give him a punch for good measure.

"Holy shit, you are possessive", Austin says smirking at the assumed possiveness.

I shake my head and say,"Or she doesn't want you touching her."

"Okay, dang", he says laughing.

"Don't touch her", I demand to him and then turn to the rest of them,"Don't."

"Got it", Austin says and then shoots her a smile. I retract my hand and Aurora grabs for my shirtsleeve. Her voice is barely a whisper when she says,"I made everything worse. I want to leave."

"It's fine. Lunch ends in three minutes okay?", I whisper back and she frowns. "Come one, tell me about the book you are reading on your phone."

"I just started it, it's called...", I watch as she gets lost in her book world and tried not to freeze at the way her hand has looped around my arm in a way she hasn't done before. The bell rings, cutting her off of telling the synopsis and she frowns.

"Continue", I tell her and she does. I smile at the way she can only talk to me when it is about her book. When she is done, I pick up her backpack and the both of us walk to her class where I drop her off with another cheeky smile.

□•□•□•□

"I feel like a burden", she admits to me when we are in my car after school before my practice. She informed me that she had to get home as soon as school was over so I jumped in the car.

I start driving toward her house,"What? Why?"

"All I do is hang off of your arm and say no words to your friends. Am I burdening you?", she asks and I let out a small chuckle.

"Anything but that, Rory. You stopped all the girls from wanting to bombard me with requests all day and it may not seem it, but I genuinely like hanging out with you", I say matching her tone and she draws her bottom lip into her mouth and I lift my eyes off of her lips so fast.

"Okay, Oliver", she says and I laugh.

"Nobody calls me Oliver. Just Oli", I say when she blinks at me in confusion.

"That's it?", she asks like it is kind of sad that I only have a shortened name as my own.

"My parents call me by my middle name: Nolan."

The light turns red and I feel her gaze on me and when I turn to her to find that she is openly staring at me. I can't say it doesn't make my body heat up especially my ears.

"You don't look like a Nolan", she says and now it is my turn to stare at her. Her eyes are so sharp that they are the first things I notice about her, her nose is long and thin it reminds of an ethnic nose, and her lips are so full it looks like she is pouting all the time. Her chin is so pointy I envy it a little as my own is a bit of a butt chin. Her cheekbones are lower than most but even then, she looks gorgeous.

"I don't look like a Nolan?", I ask her and she shrugs.

"You're Oli. The super popular and personable guy, not Nolan the serious guy", she says and I crack a smile and start driving again.

"I guess it depends on the environment. It also depends on the people", I say as I pull in to her driveway.

"Can I call you Oliver though?", she whispers and I nod. "Thank you Oliver for your kindness."

"You're welcome, Aurora."

"No", she blurts out and I stop trying to remember what I did wrong.

"Don't call me that. My full name", she says and I nod.

"Sorry", I say and she shakes her head.

"I swear I'm making such a mess. Okay I'm leaving", I say.

"Wait", I say as she starts opening the door. She turns to me and I get a clear view of her face as the hair has finally moved away. "Tomorrow is game day. Do you think you can wear my Jersey?" I try to not sound so nervous when I say it.

"Sure", she says so I let her get out of the car before reaching back and grabbing the jersey from the backseat.

"Sorry it wasn't recently washed but you can", I say and hand it to her trying to not touch her.

"It's fine", she gives me a soft smile and I wonder if she looks pretty now, how much prettier she can look when she fully smiles. Or even laughs? It makes me want to get those reactions out of her.

"Be safe. Bye", I say and she closes the door and walks toward her house, her shoulders shrinking. She turns, gives me a wave, and I drive off.

Chapter Four

A urora

The next day, I want to skip school. My dad hadn't been home when I came home yesterday, so I had made his late lunch and ran upstairs. After locking my door, I layed in bed trying to get a piece of mind. Being with Oliver is scary but I want to be there though. Oliver is the nicest guy I ever met but it does scare me that he could get abusive any second. That's why I'm not comfortable around him.

When I get comfortable with him, will he start viewing me differently?

While I'm lost in my thoughts, a loud bang on my bedroom door pulls me out of it. I let out a shaky breath and sat up in bed waiting for him to leave me alone.

"Do you think you can get a guy to scare me off?", he says and I notice the slurring of his words and know that he is drunk. When did he have the time to drink? He goes on,"A big guy in a big car, well I don't fear him."

I let him continue his tangent until he gets to the last part. "The next time I see him around here, he is going to get a peice of mind. I mean why would he even want to date you, the only thing you have going for you is your prettiness but other than that, you're nothing."

I feel my emotions move from mad to a little hurt but I shake my head. Oliver said he chose me, so I should trust him.

"Get out here", he barks out loud suddenly and I get off the bed and hold my breath when I open the door. He barged into my room and the first thing he does is make a hasty motion at grabbing me. He grabs my waist, hard and possessive, and pulls me flesh to him. I hold my gag in and he gropes my waist tighter as I try to shimmy out.

His lips meet my bare neck and I feel bile raising up my throat. "Does he treat you like I do?", he whispers against my neck and I try to tune him out.

"Let go", I say instead, which he ignores. I ball up my fists and gathering as much courage as I can and punch him. It hits sloppy on his jaw but it is enough for him to push off me. He looks up at me with a smirk and pushes me so hard, I go a few feet back. He starts to smile right before I use that to my leverage and close my door. In record time, I have locked all my locks and have fallen on the floor, with my hands helplessly to my side.

My waist hurts and there is a stinging on my neck where he tried to do whatever he did. I stay like that for so long I had fallen asleep. That's how I woke up the next morning, on the floor with my body aching. I didn't want to move, didn't want to leave the safety of my room.

But even then, I carried myself to my bathroom and did my routine before slipping into his jersey. It is sleeveless and so big it slips past my thigh. I pinch at the fabric and at my skin before I shake my head violently. I can't do this, so I go into my closet and pick out another hoodie and put that on. I throw the Jersey on top and slip into a pair for black jeans. I decide to put my hair up but when I gather my hair up, I notice the marks on my neck.

Tears threatened to come out as I cursed at him a million times. I put my hair down and use concelar to cover the mark as best as I can. What if Oliver sees this, would he think I was betraying him? I know it's fake but your girlfriend walking around with another guys mark has to be something. After a while, it dawns on me that that is what he wanted all along.

I throw on some other products on my face and rush downstairs to make him his signature omelete. I finish within ten minutes and grab my back-pack leaving early before he can wake up. I walk passed my neighborhood but then stop for a breath. My sprain is healing but is still hurts so I press my back against a building. I close my eye to take a breath until a car honks to make me open my eyes.

"Rory?", the voice says and I look ahead at the deep green jeep with Oliver inside of it. I get on my feet and he brings the car closer to me so I walk toward it. "What are you doing here?", he says and I just shrug a shoulder and head to the passenger side seat. Instead of throwing my backpack on the floor, I placed it on my belly, needing more protection today. Everything hurts.

"Are you okay?", he asks me like he did yesterday and I nod looking out the window instead.

"Rory?", he tries again and I take a deep breath in and say,"Can we just get to school already?"

He must hear the desperation in my voice as he starts the car up again and drives down my street. He passes my house in a blur and starts heading to school. A hear a low hum and my stomach churns at the unwanted noise. But when I look at him, I watch him softly tapping the steering wheel and his lips softly humming. He catches me looking and meets my eye for a second which is all it takes me to turn my head back to the front of the car.

He doesn't say anything though only hums a little louder and soon enough we are in school. He parks in the space he did previously and we both get out of the car. He holds out a hand for my backpack and I hand it to him. I walk close to him with a hand hugging my body and when I look up at him to grab his shirtsleeve, I find that he doesn't have one. He is wearing a short sleeve which I try not to notice how his arm flexes as we walk.

"Oliver?", I say hoping I'm not too quiet and he looks down at me, his hair falling in his eyes.

I point to my shirtsleeve and it takes him a few second to understand before he pulls at his shirt, trying to stretch it out. It doesn't stretch much and I shake my head. I take a step closer to him and hope that it's enough to make it seem like we are dating. Once we get in, people are looking at us and I'm falling behind Oliver with my sprained leg and the fact that his legs are naturally long. He must be at least 6"3.

Oliver stops ahead of me and I walk toward him. He smiles down at me and holding in a breath, I find his hand by his side and slip my pinky finger in his. I take in a sharp breath at the contact, so soft and I try not to notice how warm I suddenly feel. He doesn't say anything but I can see the small smile on his lip and I look down at the floor embarrassed.

He doesn't retract his finger though and starts walking. I have to tighten my finger in his in order to not lose him and we get to my first hour shortly after. I retract my finger from his in record speed and he hands me my backpack.

"I'll see you at lunch?", he asks softly and I nod. He nods once at me and then walks backwards away from me. "I'll miss you", he shouts at me loud enough for the whole hallway to hear and my heart warms a bit.

□•□•□□•

I make it to the lunch table before the guys and settle in the space we did yesterday. I'm two chapters in when their laughter brings me out of my book and I look up to see four guys heading toward me. I spot Oliver smiling the hardest and know that he was the one who told the joke, the pride evident on his face. His eyes meet mine but his smile doesn't falter, instead it has his eyes twinkling a little.

"Hey babe", he shouts walking toward the table a little faster and the guys follow him with a small smirk on their lips.

"Hi", I say softly when he drops his backpack on the table.

"Come on, let's grab lunch", he says softly and I shake my head. I haven't been able to keep down food for so long I don't even want to try. He only holds out his pinky finger and not wanting to let him look dumb, I slip mine in his. I tighten the hold and try to make all the flashbacks of my father's hand on me disappear. I open my eyes to find him looking at me and the memories blur for a second.

The lunch line is short and Oliver makes me get a brownie and a piece of pizza. The pizza makes me want to hurl and the brownie isn't any better. I take a seat at my spot and Oliver follows. The backpack in between us helps so he is not touching me and when I look up at Austin I can see he has kept a distance between us.

I give him a little nod which he smiles at me for. I look back at Oliver who has started eating his food. I try to take a bite of the pizza but my stomach lurches at it and I drop it on my plate. Instead I pull out my phone and continue reading the book I started yesterday. I'm so invested in the main characters almost kissing that I don't see the piece of brownie in front of me. I turn to Oliver who is talking to his friend but his hand stays in front of my mouth. I hold in a breath and open my mouth to take the piece. I almost graze my lips with his finger and that makes me let out a shaky breath.

He glances at me then and gives me an encouraging nod. I have my eyes on his as I chew the food but it takes a second to swallow it. Instantly I need water and drop my eyes to grab for it. But I can't find it, did I not bring water?

"Here", his voice is barely above a whisper and he has his bottle in front of me. I'm about to reach for it before he places it to my mouth leaving me no choice but to tilt my jaw and take a sip.

"Oh shit", a voice says making me move my mouth away from the bottle and toward the voice. "She has a hickey", the person in front of me says and I feel my heart beating faster.

"I uh", I stutter looking at Oliver but he only displays a fake smirk on his face and shrugs at the guys. The guys laugh and when I glance back at him, I find that he isn't looking at me anymore. Swallowing my hurt, I go back to my book but I can't as my mind is fizzled with the fact that he seems rather hurt. The bell rings and Oliver picks up my backpack but doesn't hold out his pinky finger. I do though but his eyes are on his friends so I put my hand back in my pocket. He starts walking toward my next class and I'm about to speak to him before he drops my backpack on my shoulder and leaves.

I frown not because I'm hurt but it seems that he is hurt.

Chapter Five

A urora

He is standing by his car at the end of the day when I find him again. Upon seeing me, he opens the passenger side door and holds it open for me.

"Oliver, I didn't—", I start saying but he only shakes his head.

"It's not my business", he cuts me off and I look down at the floor before getting in the car. He walks back around to his side and starts the car. I swallow and start talking again,"I swear I don't have a boyfriend or any-thing."

"So a hickey just magically showed up on your neck?", he says in a voice higher than he ever used with me and I try not to cower away at it.

"I swear, Oliver. It's not a hickey", I say and he turns to me at the red light.

"Let me see it?", he asks and I shake my head. He only makes a sound of disapproval and I hold in a breath before pulling down the hood of the hoodie. He skims my neck and then nods once.

"Whatever. Just that, I want to know if you do have a boyfriend. We can break this up", he says and I shake my head.

"You're the first guy who ever talked to me", I whisper so softly he doesn't hear me.

"What?", his hazel eyes lighter in the sunshine.

"You're the first guy who ever talked to me", I say and his eyes widen at my admission.

"No way", he says and the light turns green so he drives.

"Well, a guy who came up to me on his own", I amend and he repeats his previous statement and I let out a sound I wasn't aware of. Was it a chuckle?

He glances at me and it lets me know that he heard me also. A little smile stretches out his face and I avert my gaze, my cheeks heating up.

"So when does the game start?", I ask him as we near my house.

"7 but I have to be here half an hour earlier so I'll come pick you up at 6", he says pulling into my driveway.

"Okay, but don't honk", I say to him and grab my backpack and open the door.

"Later, Rory", he says softly and I nod at him.

□•□•□•□

Getting out of the house a few hours later is a harder battle than I'd thought. I kept waiting for him to go to his room, but he stayed downstairs laughing at something playing on the television. I had covered the hickey again with more concealer so it doesn't show anymore. I pulled my hair up in a ponytail and my natural hair wavy down my back. I had pulled the jersey off but then realizing that it's his game I put it back on. After looking in the mirror, I found myself looking a little tired.

I put on a little bit of makeup and after looking in the mirror again I saw that I looked presentable. I sneaked a peek downstairs at around 6 and saw my dad staring at the television intently and so I took in a big breath and walked past him. Once I got to the door, I opened it and slipped out before hearing him cursing at me.

I just hoped that when I came back, the alcohol he was drinking would knock him out.

□•□•□•□•□•

Oliver had gotten to the school half an hour earlier but there were so many people in the gym already. With my finger in his, he led us to the front seats and said,"Sit here."

"So close to the court?", I whispered and he nodded. He started to slip his finger out of mine but I held on tighter and said,"I'm scared."

"Of what, Rory?", he asks soflty and I shake my head.

"I don't know anybody", I admit.

"You know me. Just keep looking for me on the court and that would be good. But oh don't read your book", he says scratching his head and I frown.

"No girlfriend of mine would be invested in their book while coming to watch my game. Can you try?", he asks and I look up at his body. His arms flex with anything he does and the jersey makes the skin it's exposing stand out.

"I guess", I say, bringing my eye back up to his eye and he nods, slipping his finger out of mine and right before he gets out of my sight, he pulls the shirt up a little. I warm up a little but when he looks back at me with a knowing smirk, my entire body flames up. I hear his laughter down the hallway before he disappears down the locker rooms.

After about ten minutes, an older couple shows up beside me. I look up to meet a woman in her 40s and a man with his hand in hers. I move away to let them go through and they both sit right beside me. I narrow my eyes but ignore them.

"Hey", the woman says to me and I turn to her. She glances at my jersey and then at her husband. "That's an official jersey if I've ever seen one", the guy says and I have the sudden urge to take it off.

"Are you our son's girlfriend?", the woman asks and I feel regret at the thoughts that were going through my head. Are these Oliver's parents?

"I knew Nolan had a girl", the guy says with a soft chuckle and the woman joins in.

"What's your name, honey?", she asks me and I try to not make my voice so small when I answer.

"Rory", the woman repeats and then she shares a nod with her husband. "I've never seen you before", she says and I nod.

"This is", I start and then try again, "Not really my scene."

"Basketball?", she asks and I nod even though I meant the crowd.

"How long have you guys been dating?", she asks me and I try to rake my head around a lie before we hear someone running toward us.

"Mom, Dad", the guy says enthusiastically at the couple beside me and I look at him. I watch as he hugs both of his parents and as well as a kiss on the cheek for his mom. His dad slaps a hand around his shoulder and he says, "Are we winning this game?"

"I have to. I heard that scouts are coming next week", he says and I can hear that he sounds nervous.

"You'll do great", his parents say at the same time. They share a laugh but his mom recovers faster and turns to me.

"When were you going to tell us about your girlfriend?", she says, smiling wide. Oliver looks down at me and then at the jersey I wear. He smirks as if it's the first time he has noticed it and I avert my gaze. I pull up the hood of my hoodie trying to cower away.

"Well, we have been dating for less than a month, right babe?", he says looking at me and I nod. The fake nickname makes my heart beat pick up but I swallow it down, not wanting to feed into it.

"She's so quiet", his mom says to him and Oliver nods.

"She is but not totally. She is more talkative with me", Oliver says and his dad laughs.

"I would hope so, Nolan. Or else it would be as if all you guys did was kiss all day", his dad says already laughing at the end and my cheeks heat up. Oliver has yet to touch me unless it was me who initiated it so imagining him kissing me, with a hand under my jaw makes my heart skip a beat. I glance up at him and find that his ears are flushed as well.

"Well I have to get going", he says and then hugs his parents goodbye again. He stops in front of me and I watch as he extends a slow hand in front of me and touch his jersey I'm wearing. I want to cower away even though he has yet to touch me.

"Sorry", he whispers at me and then says, louder,"Look for me on the court, baby." He leaves with a wink at me and I feel my head dizzying. His parents laugh as he runs off into the court. His mom turns to me,"He is very gentle with you."

I only nod and she continues,"I like seeing him so kind."

I agree with her, nodding and then train my eye at the number 15. He is currently placing a white headband on his forehead in order to stop the hair come toward his eye. I watch as he talks with Austin, the both of them animated.

There is a loud music and I watch as the marching band walks out at the signaling the game starting.

□•□•□•□•

"You were amazing", his mom shouts as soon as he makes it back to us. His dad congratulates him with a hand outstretched in front of him. I watch as he hugs both of his parents again with a feeling I hadn't felt in a while. When was the last time I willingly hugged my parents? My mom has been dead for a few years now and my dad....God, my breath hitches at the thought. I suddenly feel more dizzy than I did earlier and the noise around me has multiplied.

I can't do this, I can't be here. I frantically look around at the quickest exists and start to head to it when I hear my name being called. I look back, a tear almost falling out of my eye, to Oliver who is starting to frown.

"Babe, what's wrong?", he asks and I close my eye willing the noise to die down a little. It doesn't, instead it gets louder.

"I don't feel so good", I admit in a whisper and he makes his way toward me with hasty steps.

"When did you last eat?", he asks and I watch as he retracts his hand. I hope I didn't flinch at that. I don't answer and he curses under his breath. "Don't tell me it was the tiny piece of brownie I fed you." He follows my eye and upon seeing it, he curses a little louder.

"Rory, why", he starts but then cuts himself off,"Actually let's just get you home." He starts walking toward the exit but a few people calling his name stops him. He looks back at them and Austin shouts,"Aren't you going to celebrate with us?"

"My girlfriend doesn't feel too good. I have to get her home", he says his voice frantic and I feel a ping of guilt at the fact that I'm making him miss out on his victory.

"Oh, Rory. Are you okay?", Austin shouts at me and I can't get myself to respond in any way. Oliver looks down at me and then says to Austin,"Can you help gather my stuff? We can celebrate tomorrow."

"Sure", Austin says and Oliver holds out his pinky which I take but it's not enough for me to keep his pace. Instead, I place my hand on his shirt, stretching it out but he doesn't seem to notice as he leads us out to the parking lot. He finds his car and we start heading to it. Once I get into his car, he heads over too and then glances at me. He looks worried so I shake my head.

"I'm fine", I say.

I'll be fine.

He doesn't respond and instead drives out the parking lot and toward my house. But when we are almost at my house, he takes a wrong turn and I sit up to look out the window. I glance at him and find that his eyes are trained on the road and that his leg is bouncing up and down.

He makes a quick turn and I almost jerk forward. "Sorry", he whispers before driving a little faster and then pulls up at a window.

"10 count of chicken nuggets and a large fry please. And water", Oliver says not waiting for the woman to ask him. The woman tells him to move forward and I shake my head.

"I don't want to eat", I whisper.

"You have to", he says and I notice how worried he sounds. I claw at my jersey and he looks at me.

"What's wrong?", he says and I ball up my fists.

"I don't, I want to go to sleep", I say moving restlessly.

"I'll take you straight home after you eat. Come on, Rory", he says softly and I'm about to object when he stops at a window and the woman hands him a bag as well as a cup of water. He thanks her and hands her the bill before pulling out of the driveway and parking in the lot.

"Here", he hands me the bag and then places the straw on my mouth. I want to object but then my mouth opens up and I start chugging the water like I've never had water. The cool waters feels so good I'm about to get some more, but he pulls it away.

I look up at him, frowning, but he only points to the bag on my lap. I shake my head but he only places the water on the cup holder and grabs the bag out of my lap. He pulls out a red container of fries and places one at my lip. The smell makes my stomach lurch but he only leaves it there.

"I, I can't", I start but he shakes his head.

"You may think your body is wanting to reject it but it is craving it. Do your stomach a favor, Rory", he says and my stomach growls at his words. I sigh and take a bite of the fry but he stuffs the whole thing in my mouth. I chew and this time it's easier. I swallow and feel my body wanting to relax. Oliver nods and hands me more fries. I obey him and eat a few. He hands me the chicken nuggets and I manage to eat a few before pushing it toward him.

"A little more", he says softly and hands me the French fry. I nod and place a few more in my mouth. He starts the car and reverses it as he starts heading to my house. I look at him and then grab a few fries before placing it in front of his face. He glances down at it and then at me. I raise my eyebrow and he opens his mouth. I push it into his mouth and retract my hand before he can make contact with my skin. I manage to eat a few more chicken nuggets before downing the rest of the water.

I feel instantly lighter and I can't help but feel grateful for him. He pulls into my driveway and parks the car. I look out the window and see that none of the lights are in my house, that means he has passed out before sundown.

"Thank you, Oliver", I say to him, hoping to sound sincere. His eyes soften and I feel like I should reach out and touch him. But the thought of him reciprocating makes me flinch so I don't.

"You're welcome, Rory. Have a good weekend", he says and I open the door.

"You too, Oliver", I say and head over to my house. Before I get in though, I turn around and say,"You played so well, by the way."

"I know", he says smirking,"From the way you were only ever staring at me."

I narrow my eyes on his cockiness but then wave and he drives off.

Chapter Six

O liver

It is the day after our basketball game against one of our rivals and since we won, we are celebrating today. Typically, it would've been last night, but with Rory about to pass out, we had to postpone it. It's the next day and the party is hosted at my house with my parents here. They say that if we are going to drink, they have to be here, so the team takes a seat on my couch and we start drinking.

I take a swig of my beer, and say, "We have to train hard next week. A scouts coming."

"Really?", Austin asks and I nod. The team cheers, most of us loud only a handful of them don't care about this sort. But I do, I love this and if I don't get a future in this, I'd probably be lost. Basketball has been all I've known, ever since I started playing in the little league at the age of four. I have to have a future in this and if that means more training then so be it.

"Four practice instead of two", Jake, a guy on the team says and I nod. It's going to be tough.

"I'll have to drop of Rory first though", I say feeling a little tilt in my head with the drink.

"I don't understand her", Jake says and a few others agree. I feel my sudden need to defend her surface and before long I'm saying "How so?""

Austin glances at the team and then sets his eye on me,"She's so quiet and even though she clings to you, she never touches you."

"So?", I ask before realizing by myself how it seems. "Yeah but in public. She's much more relaxed with me in private." It was true enough.

Jake chuckles taking another swig of the beer,"Making out in public is one thing, but holding hands is another. I think I've noticed a pinky hold and that's it. Kind of lame."" The team barks out a laugh and I feel my anger rising.

"You're noticing quite a lot now aren't you, Jakey?", I say my voice unkind.

"She's just weird. Flinching at our every word, at our accidental touch. She seems to not like us." The adjective used to describe her makes me want to slap the drink out of his hand.

"She doesn't have to like you. She likes Austin", I say a little envious at my last statement.

"She does?"Austin asks with a grin and I nod.

"She feels at ease with you, I can see that." Austin lets out a whoop and then clinks his drink with mine. We all quiet down, me glaring at our teammates and them looking down at the floor. We hear some noises from upstairs and I groan.

"Mom, Dad, not when I'm home. Much less my team!", I shout at them and my friends laugh knowingly. I pinch the bridge of my nose and exhale.

"Nobody is shitting on my girl anymore, got it?", I tell them once we all calm down and I wait for all of them to nod invidually.

□•□•□•□•

The next Monday, I get to Rory's house at 7:15 as opposed to 7 on the dot and find her waiting a block from her street. I wonder if she decided to walk to school. I pull up next to her and watch as she walks toward my car, her leg better. I'm glad for that. She gets in and grimaces and I feel the need to ask her if she is okay even though I know that she wouldn't answer.

"Good morning", I say instead and she looked at me. She is dressed in a similar outfit as all of last week, a sweater and black baggy jeans. She takes the hood off of her head and her full head of blonde curls falls down her back. She is the opposite of me, all lighter features as opposed to my jet black hair and hazel eyes. Her eyes are green, so light in the morning I'm afraid she can see through me.

"Morning", she mumbles and I let out a chuckle before starting to drive. She only lives a couple minutes away from my house,, so picking her up is no problem.

Once we get to the school, I park and Rory gets up to leave but I stop her by caling her name. She turns to me and just before I have the thought of her hair covering her face, she tucks it behind her ear. I try not to get surprised at how much it assunciates her features.

"So I was talking to my team and they don't believe we are dating", I say not adding the mean comment being said about her. I'm still kind of pissed off at my team for their insensitive comments. She glances at me and then at the people outside of the car, who are rushing to get to class.

"Um", she says and tucks her hands underneath her leg. I glance at it and then get the courage to say,"You can hold my hand." She looks up at me panicky and I feel ashamed for asking her that. She brings her hands out from underneath her and extends it toward me. I take notice of the way it shakes.

"Nevermind, we don't have to", I start and she ignores me by placing it gently on top of mine. Her touch is so light I have to concentrate in order to fel it. I look down at her and find her taking a shaky breath in, and my heart pings at her raw emotions. I flip my hand from under hers so our palms can touch and when try do, I notice how small her hand is. I open my fingers and hers fall right in before I interlock them. She releases another breath and I watch the way she is studying our hands. Her eyebrows furrowed in thought and she retracts her hand from mine. I miss its warmth already but she looks away from me and opens up the door. Right, we are almost late to our first class.

I open up my dor and get out as well. She meets me in front of my car and I start walking toward the building. Once we are in, her hand slide into mine and she copies the way I interlocked pir fingers together. I look down at her with an encouraging smile and she only looks at me.

"Promise your hand is not going to travel any her else", she whispers and I squeeze our hand together in answer. A slow smile plays on her face and I want to take the time to memorize it, instead, the first bell rings and we have to rush to get to class on time. I leave her again with a cheeky smile.

••••

"I like your hair", Austin says to my fake girlfriend as we begin eating. I forced her to get something and she chose fries which I am not surprised at. Rory looks around at the others and then runs a finger through a lock of hair so silky. Austin nods at her and she blushes. Actually blushes, her cheeks becoming pink and then she smiles at him. I want to get her to do that, I think. She pops a fry in her mouth and I smile at that.

"So what book are you planning on reading next?", I ask her and she looks up at me in thought.

"As long as you love me", she says and I swear my heart beat picks up.

"Pardon?", I ask her and she looks up at me funny.

"That's the name of the book", she says and I let out a little chuckle. She shakes her head again and looks at her phone.

"Don't start the book now", I say to her. She frowns but reluctanely nods, putting her phone away. "Tomorrow", I whisper to her and she nods once more. She spends the rest of the lunch hour trying to catch up on the conversation being had. After the bell rings, she stands up close to me and slips her hand inine and I tell myself to not like it so much.

□•□•□•

Practice is brutally long and afterwards, Austin asks for a ride.

"Okay, yeah, but I have to stop by a bookstore really quickly", I say to him and his eyes widen in surprise. "For Rory", I add and he nods. He gives my cheek a little pat and says,"Look at you being very lovey dovey." I shake him off and get in the car. The closest bookstore is ten minutes away so we make it there in no time. I get in and go on the hunt for the book. I find it under the new release section and eyes slightly widen at the cover. I smirk and pick it up. I also pick up two more similar ones and walk to the checkout. After buying the books, I smile at the fact that I cannot wait to see her reaction.

"Did she ask for these?", Austin asks picking up the books while I start driving. I shake my head and say,"No, it's a surprise."

"Aww, you are being such a cute boyfriend", he says and I abruptly stop the car to make him jerk forward. He looks at me with a hand on his heart and I let out a small chuckle.

"Not too much", I say to him and he nods. I nod in agreement but it's not long before he starts singing a love song to me.

"Oh my god", I groan and he laughs. He continues to sing all the way to his house.

"Stop flirting with her", I say as he gets out of the car.

"Huh", he asks genuinely confused.

"Lunch", I say, my answer short, and watch as his brain finds the memory. "I was just paying her a compliment", he says and I shake my head.

"She's my girl to compliment, go get your own", I mumble and he laughs. I close the door in his face and drive off. I still hear his laugh though and shake my head as I drive to my own house.

Chapter Seven

A urora

There is something that is making Oliver smile the whole drive to school. It couldn't be me as I've been sulking in pain from what I've endured this morning. I hadn't made my father's breakfast earlier enough that he used me as a personal punching bag. He was smart enough to not hit me on my face except for the slap that didn't hurt as bad as the rest of the punches thrown on me. My ribs hurt and even though I'm trying to stay calm, my heart is violently racing in my chest.

I wish that Oliver's happiness would transfer to me but he doesn't say anything to me until after the drive is over. "I've got something for you", he says right after parking and killing the engine. I unbuckle my seatbelt and turn to him,"Yes?" I really wish my voice wasn't so small, that I was stronger than this.

But I'm not.

He reaches forward and I think he is going to touch me, but he heads to the backseat and I hear him rummage for something. He pulls back, makes eye contact for me for a second his eyes so much lighter with the sun shining, and then moves back to his seat. I try not to think of how close he was to me, and how I didn't hate it. His smile is even more bigger now, the dimples making an appreance and then he hands me a plastic bag. I take it from him with uncertaintly and when I look inside, tears form in my eye.

I put my hand inside and pull out the book he asked me about yesterday. I hold it up to him and the events from earlier this morning and his kindness right now makes a tear flow out of my eye. He noticed it before I wipe it off and frowns.

"Oliver, I", I start saying but when I look back in the bag, there are two more. I take those out as well, and my heart flutters from happiness. This is exactly what I needed, fluffy romance filled novels. I hold the books up to my chest and give him a big smile. "I love them", I say and I watch as his eyes soften.

"Why were you crying then?", he asks and I peer through the books to learn more about them.

"Had a rough morning and your kindness was overbearing", I admit in a whisper, my eyes still scanning through the books.

"You're welcome, Rory", he says so tenderly I look up to find him studying me.

"No, this is just like the best thing you could've ever done for me", I say my voice a little louder. I watch as his face morphs into something modest before he glances away from me. Is he blushing? I take a little pride in that but I'm not allowed to enjoy it as he opens his door and starts walking out.

I grab my bag, my books, and head out of the car as well. He meets me by his car side, and I look up to see his cheeks still a little flushed. He glances down at me and says, "Bag."

"No I've got it today", I say but he still puts his hand out and I reluctantly hand him it. Now, I'm able to read the back of the books for their synopsis. I'm reading them as we walk in and I hear him grunt beside me. Putting the books underneath my arm, I turn to him, "What is it?"

His voice is loud when he says,"No, I just thought that buying you books would make you appreciate me more instead of ditching me to read in the hallway, babe." The use of the nickname tells me that he said it for the intended purpose for the girls swarming around us to listen.

"Oh", I say softly and walk close to him and place my hand in his. He intertwines them and then a smile appears on his face. I hear a couple of positive murmurs around me and they match my internal thoughts. The encounter made me forget that this was fake for a second. Still, I clutch my new gifted books and we head to my first class.

□•□•□□••

"No, I'm telling you, the game is going to have to go perfect. I need the scouts to look at us", Oliver is enunciating to his team as they are complaining about the practices for the week. I'm reading my book with a hand on Oliver's as he has put it on the table for everyone to see. I'm playing with his fingers as I tune the rest of their conversation out and into the book I'm reading.

I'm so invested in it that I don't comprehend anything until after I hear a click of a camera.

Automatically my heart beat picks up but when I find Oliver's phone propped up toward his chest, I relax. I look at him and he clicks another picture. I bury my face back in the book in an attempt to hide but he only clicks a few more pictures. I pick up his index finger and bend it so far he hisses in pain.

"What was that for?", he says but I only feign innocence and I rub my hand on his.

"What were all the pictures for?"I ask and he places his phone in front of me and when I press on the screen it's me looking up from my book, a small smile on my face, and my hand in his. A lock of hair is in my face but my eyes are showing for the most part. I stare at the picture for a moment before sliding his phone back to his.

"And that's your wallpaper?", I whisper and he nods. "Why?"

"Because I have to have my girlfriend looking back at me everytime I touch my phone", he says and his loud voice makes me know that he again intended for people to hear. Is our relationship not convincing that he needs to make it aware? A couple of his friends chuckle and when I turn to Austin he is smiling at me.

"You know he has a point", Austin says,"They guy calls you his girl every chance he gets."

His girl.

The phrase is something I can't comprehend. I glance at Oliver who is again blushing and he reaches past me and gives his friend a punch on the shoulder. "Shut up", he murmurs and then looks back at me.

"My girl", I test out the words on my tongue silently and it makes me kind of smile. He takes back his phone and goes through the photos again before setting it on the table. I touch his screen to find the same photo displayed on the phone. I give him a small smile before pulling out my old beat up phone and snapping a picture of him. In the photo, he is looking at me with curiosity and yet intensity in his eye, his lips tilted up like it's natural and his hair falling right above his eye.

I set the photo as my wallpaper and he presses the screen to look at it. I watch as a small smile spreads across his face and he murmurs something under his breath.

"What?", I ask and he looks at me with a smirk.

"You look like my girl", he says softly and yet a little loud and I hear a couple whoops from his friends. I look down and hope that my face isn't as red as it feels. I feel the warmth through my whole body. When I look up at him though, his smirk tells me that my face is red against my pale skin.

□•□□•□•

Oliver informs me that our ride back home has to be quickened every day for this week as he has to get to practice earlier. That also means that he is quiet during the car ride probably thinking about the plays in his head. He pulls into my driveway and I get out of the car.

"You know, Oliver", I start before closing the door behind me,"You don't have to worry that much. You play really well."

"Playing well is different than playing best", he says not unkindly but a little faraway.

"And you need to play the best?", I ask. He looks at me and makes a face like it should've never been a question.

"The scouts aren't looking for rookies. They are looking for players who can earn them wins every single time. They need the best person if they are going to invest in them", he says and I nod, drawing my bottom lip in my mouth.

"Well, you are good. So..", I play with the straps of my backpack.

"Thank you, Rory", he says smiling at me and I smile back at him. I close the door behind me and head over to my house, not bothering to wave back because I find myself staring at my dad in the window. He looks pissed and I sigh knowing that I'm not going to get a free card today.

"You're still with that guy?", he barks at me as he opens the door and I try not to shrink in front of him. I only manage to nod and he laughs in my face. I keep my face on the ground and hear him say,"He'll leave you soon enough."

I don't say anything and he steps back laughing a little more. I start walking toward my room and think I succeeded in avoiding him but his hand slaps my butt makes me close my eyes in disgust.

I thought I would be able to escape.

Chapter Eight

Oliver

It's game day.

I'm in the locker room an hour earlier trying to come up with a way to feel the most confident and yet step out of my comfort zone. I need to focus on the game and not on the scout I know is going to be sitting right above Rory once we are near the game. I claw at my jersey once it gets too hot and take it off trying to cool off. This time Rory wanted to stay at the school before the game which worked perfectly for me since I couldn't be under a wheel today. After what felt like a good hour, I hear my teammates enter the locker room.

"Oli", I hear a shout and look up at Austin who is looking at me with the biggest smile on his face. I glare at him for his sudden excitment when I am barely trying to keep it together. He steps off to the side and I find Rory behind him. Except, she looks so much more different today. She is wearing my jersey but with a crewneck underneath as opposed to a hoodie and her hair is down past her shoulders as usual. What makes my heart skip a beat is the number 15 written on her cheek, so glittery it shines against the flouracent lights.

"What happened?"I ask, slipping on my jersey but not before noticing the way she looked at my bare chest for a second before turning her head away. Austin smiles at me,"She came to show you her look for you."

I look past him to the girl beside him and she shrugs. The number on her cheek catches my eye again and I press my lips together in a thin line in order to not smile at her.

"Go away, let me talk to her", I tell Austin who is staring at the two of us. He doesn't make a point to move and I give him a look. He steps back and further into the lockeroom. I walk past her and hope that she follows me out.

"Hi", she says to me once we are out of the locker room and in the hallway where I can hear the crowd already.

"Hey", I say suddenly nervous, I've never felt this way around a girl. She doesn't say anything else and I eye the number again. "You did that your-self?", I ask and she shakes her head.

"Your mom showed up early and saw me. And then she had a cheerleader do this for me", she says nervously.

"No, I love it", I say softly and watch as her eyes soften at the compliment. I reach out my hand and hope that she will slip it in mine. She does and I feel myself calm down.

"Sorry if my hand is clammy, I'm so nervous for this game", I admit and she shakes her head, tightening her hold on my hand. I feel the sudden urge to take a step and put my arm around her. Only, I can't do that knowing she doesn't feel comfortable around me.

Yet, I hope.

"You're going to do great. I've been hearing your name around the halls since freshman year, you got this", she says slowly.

"Thank you", I tell her and a couple of girls walk past us so I add,"Babe." She glances at the girls and her eyes stay on one girl when she takes a step closer and tiptoes up to me. She still cannot reach me, so I crouch down a little and she whispers,"That girl doesn't like me." She steps back down, but I stay crouching and look behind her at the girl. She is a brunette staring right at us unabashedly. When she spots me looking at her, she grins so wide I can see all her gums.

"She's just jealous", I whisper to the girl with my number on her cheek.

"I don't like the attention", she admits and I nod squeezing her hand for comfort.

"It'll die down", I glance up at the digital clock on the wall and say,"I have to go." Her hand slips out of mine and she steps back a step, readying to leave.

"You'll do great", her voice is soft and she attempts to be louder when she points to her cheek and says,"I'm rooting for you."

I laugh at her sudden cheesiness and wave at her. She smiles a little at me and then turns around and leaves. I watch her retreat and tell myself that if that girl can gain a little more confidence, then so can I.

□•□□•□•□•

We are down to thirty seconds on the clock with our team winning by ten points. I know that that is really good, but I need to make a point for myself. Austin passes me the ball and I dribble it up a few feets before shooting it straight for the hoop. It hits the back of the hoop first and then starts spinning on the rim of the hoop to end up falling off instead of through. I feel my ears warm up as I hear the disappointed crowd with mixture of a negative crowd.

The timer buzzes as soon as Austin picks up the ball and I look up at the crowd to find the scout that showed up as soon as the game started. He looks at me, writes something on his clipboard, and walks away with a shake of his head. I feel my face morph in embarrassment and head straight for the locker room to try and block it out.

I hear my name a couple of times, my teammates wanting to know where I am running off to but I ignore them as I open the door and walk in. As soon as the door closes behind me, the sound deafens out and I'm alone with my thoughts. Why did he shake his head and leave? I knew I needed to make an impression but that wasn't one I was counting on.

After a couple of minutes, I have gone over every other scenario. How it could've gone. But the reality pokes up in my mind and I punch the locker beside me. The force of it isn't too hard but a gasp makes me turn my head to the sound. I find Rory standing there with shock on her face as she starts backing out of the room. I feel instant regret and am about to head for her but my parents are standing beside her.

"Nolan, what's wrong?", my dad asks me as he walks over to me and places his hands on my shoulder. I look up at my dad and feel like an absolute child, so I stand up. Now I have a few inches on him but the feeling is still present. I shake my head and he brings me in for a hug. My mom shakes her head and joins in on the hug also.

"I wanted to do better. To stand out", I tell them in the hug and they both hum in agreement. I made the scout leave as he shook his head, how? I'm mad at myself and when I look at Rory, the feeling intensifies as she stands there looking uncertain. I let go of the hug and walk toward my supposed girlfriend, wiping my face with the hem of my shirt. She starts backing up and I furrow my eyebrows in confusion.

"Babe?", I ask loud enough for my parents to hear and she still walks backwards. I stop walking and she stops also.

"I", she starts and I give her a nod of encouragement but she stops talking. She glances past me to the lockers and then at my knuckles that are just a tiny bit red.

She shakes her head and turns around and makes a beeline toward the back exit of the school. It goes to the parking lot and I follow her looking back at my parents and giving them a nod. I find her by my car heaving a few breaths.

"Are you okay?", I say starting to reach for her but she moves her hands away instead hugging herself. Is she afraid of me?

"Are you?", I start and then look away when I say,"Are you afraid of me?"

"Why?", she asks so softly I don't think she is talking to me. "Why did you suddenly have to turn so violent?", she says a little louder and her words make me back away a little.

"I'm not", I say and she shakes her head biting her bottom lip. I want to reach for her hand but I don't. Instead I say,"Rory, I promise I'm not." She doesn't say anything but glance at my knuckles again. I shake it off and put it close to her,"I'd never hit you. Do you think I'd hit you?"

She backs away and I feel a ping of disappointment pass through me at the realization that she is afraid of me.

How can she be afraid of me? I don't want her to be scared of me.

"Do you think I'd hit you?", I ask her again a little louder and she flinches at my words. Actually flinches. My entire body sags at the moment.

Who hurt her enough to make her afraid of me?

"Rory", I start slowly and say,"I promised you I'd never touch you unless you initiated it and I plan on keeping that promise. I'd never lay a hand on you."

"But", she says and her bottom lip juts out in a small pout. "You punch things when you are angry. How long until you start punching me?"

Aurora

My heart pings once again at her words and what they mean underneath it. Someone has been hurting her. And the pain is so raw that she associates it with everything she experiences.

"Rory?", I ask her and she looks up at me slowly. "I'd never hurt you, you have to believe that." I wait for her to make a sign, any sign, but she avoids my eye and looks at the ground instead.

"I promise you", I say to her and she looks up at me. "Have I ever broken a promise I made to you?", I ask her gently. "I have had every urge to pull you into a hug, to touch you, but I haven't. I don't touch you until you want me to and I'll follow that rule until you don't need for me to anymore. As for violently laying a hand on you? I would never. Believe me."

Her eyes soften and a tear falls out of her eye and I want to wipe it off. She nods once and I feel my shoulders sag in relief. "Say it, Rory."

"I trust you, Oliver", she whispers.

"Good girl", I say and then curse myself for choosing those two words but she doesn't make any indication of disliking it. "Now, I have to pick up our trophy and stuff, do you want to go back with me or sit in my car?"

She looks around at my car and then at me. Her eyes flash of sudden concern and she shakes her head. "Go with you", she says just the three words. She holds out her hand and slips it in mine and the both of us walk back inside the building.

With my hand in hers, we head to the court where a trophy is being handed to my team. Austin grabs it and walks over to me with a grin,"We did it, Oli." I laugh at his words and walk closer to him. Austin glances at me and then to Rory, down to our hands and groans. I raise my eyebrow at him prompting him to explain.

"You guys couldn't wait ten minutes?", he asks and his words automatically register in my mind but when I look down at Rory she is looking at me in confusion.

I crouch down and whisper in her ear,"He asummes we went out there to make out." I pull away from her and watch as her face heats up, her pale face reddening. I slap Austin on the back and he smirks looks down at the girl beside me.

"Is he a good kisser?", Austin ask and Rory reddens further and I slap him on the neck this time. I grab the trophy out of his hand and hold it up and turn to the stadium. The crowd cheers loudly and I also hold up the hand holding Rory and they cheer even louder now.

She flushes red and I pull her hand down. I hand Austin the trophy and say to him,"I'll see you at the party." I take her out of the court and toward the locker room.

"Do you want to come to the party?", I ask her and she shakes her head.

"I'm exhausted but you enjoy yourself, okay?", she says and I nod. We walk to my car and she says,"You did so good. Don't beat yourself up about it."

"Thank you, Rory", I say and she smiles at me the number catching my eye again.

"I like my number on you", I say.

"Just drive", she says and I laugh so loud she cracks a smile. It seems that the energy between us has been rekindled.

Chapter Nine

A urora

Towards the end of the next week, Oliver tells me that his parents want to have dinner with me on Sunday. I shake my head looking out the window. On the weekends, my dad does not have work so the chances of me attempting to sneak out of the house is low. I honestly don't want to get out of my room on the weekends and rather stay holed up in my room with a few books and some snacks. Best to stay off the radar on those days.

"I'm busy on the weekends", I tell him and he hums.

"Okay, today is Friday so we will have to reschedule it for next week. My parents don't have work on Tuesday. Does that work for you?"

"Sure after school", I say and he shakes his head.

"I have practice, so you'll have to wait at school and then we can go to my house", he says, turning to me at a red light.

"Sure", I say, avoiding his eyes. Over the course of the week, Oliver has been so gentle and honest with me that it has me in a dangerous position. He is getting way too close to me. And that scares me.

"Okay then", he says and gives me a too big of a grin.

□•□•□•□

Oliver has a nice home; big and every inch of it is decorated. It isn't minimalist but rather homey. Every wall in the living room has a memory of Oliver, with photos and old hand made pictures he made. It makes my heart warm at the fact that his parents treasure him so much. His mom meets us at the front entrance with a big smile and open arms.

"Oh", I say when she pulls me into a hug. It feels odd hugging Oliver's mother not having hugged him yet. I do wonder how it would be to hug him. He has a good shoulder, bulky and his arms are look so strong, I wonder what kind of protection it would provide me. She pulls away after a second and then turns to her son.

"She is so pretty, Nolan", she says and Oliver smiles at her.

"She is", he agreed and his mother beamed at that. She leads us toward the living room and tells us that his father is still upstairs showering and that he will be down in a while.

"I love all the memories of you on the walls", I say and Oliver groans.

"No, they never take it down. In fact, every week they seem to find something more embarrassing to put on the wall."

"They love you", I say a little envious at the fact that I don't have parental figures who would love me unconditionally. Oliver nods and spends the rest of the time talking about every memory on the wall. He talks like his parents don't matter that much to him, but judging by the enormous smile on his face, I can tell that he loves them so much more than he wants to lead on.

Nolan's mother, Victoria, calls us down from the kitchen that the food is ready. As we walk past the living room and toward the dining room, the smell gets stronger. We stop in the dining room and Oliver pulls out a chair for me to sit in. I sit down and he moves away and takes a seat beside me.

"Aren't you two adorable", his mom quips walking into the room with a dish which she places on the table. "Your father is still not here?"

"No", Oliver answers even though she meant it to be a rhetorical question. I chuckle under my breath and he gives me a look.

"Simon", his mother yells so loud I wouldn't think her voice could raise that high. "Get down here. Nolan's girlfriend's here."

"Coming", says a gruffly voice as we hear steps coming from the staircase. His father walks into the dining room and heads straight for his wife. He places a kiss on her forehead and then turns to us.

"Good Evening, Rory, was it?", he asks me and I nod.

"Evening, Mr. Baker", I say polietly and Oliver says his greetings as well. The family converses so easily that I instantly feel comfortable around them.

Once we get started on dinner, his mom starts asking me questions. "So tell me about your family", she says and I feel my legs moving up and down. She gives me an encouraging smile so I take a deep breath in and say,"I have an older sister who is in her second year of university. And uh my mom, she sadly passed away a few years ago, four to be exact, and so it's just my dad and I."

"Oh I'm sorry to hear that", both of the parents say and Oliver frowns at me. I ignore his eyes and settle in front of the food I've been toying around on my plate.

"Okay, you have a beauty I can't place, are you—"

"Italian", I say. "My mom was born in Italy."

"Oh", his mom says like it answers all her questions.

"Do you know Italian?", his father asks me and I nod.

"Fluently?", Oliver asks me and I nod.

"My mom made us go back there every year since my sister turned three so we picked up the language", I say softly. They all nod at me and the questions stop for a while. Oliver points to his plate and I know what he is trying to tell me. But I can't get myself to pick up the fork and eat a little.

Oliver frowns and extends his fork up to my lip and sensing eyes on me, I open my mouth and take the food. His eyes are on me as I chew and then attempt to swallow. He doesn't look away and so I swallow it and automatically I feel like I want to throw up. I look away from Oliver and to his parents. His mom is cooing while his dad has a small smile on his face. I hope they don't think I'm weird for having Oliver have to feed me.

To cover up any suspicions, I try to eat a piece of his mothers well done chicken and it takes me a good minute to swallow. I used to love food but now that I've grown distant from them, my body started rejecting the food. Oliver holds out his hand underneath the table and I place mine in his. He gives our hand a gentle squeeze so I take his support and attempt to eat more of the food.

In the end, I only ate almost half of my food, but Oliver smiled at me like I ate everything. I wonder what he must think of me, someone who has to be forced to eat. His parents shared a few stories about Oliver, Nolan as they call him, throughout dessert which Oliver asked to share claiming that he was too full. In reality it was because he wanted to feed me and couldn't if I had my own, which he wanted me to eat.

"Rory is short for something isn't it?", his mom says as we start walking out of the dining room.

"Aurora", I say nodding and his mother beams.

"Gosh that name is so pretty", she comments and I remember the first day when Oliver said that. It dawned on me now that he was so similar to his parents in a good way. She walks us toward the front door and then says to Oliver,"Don't stay out too late."

"I won't", he answers back to her and she leaves us. I start heading toward his car and he follows. We stay in park though and I grow worried.

"Oliver?", I ask and he turns to me and I swear his frown is so prominent.

"Why didn't you tell me your mom had passed away?", he asks me which surprises me.

"Well", I play with his radio station,"It never came up." He glances at my actions and frowns deeper.

"We've known each other for over a month, I'd like to know more about you", he says and I frown.

"You do know a lot about me."

"Like what?", he asks serious.

"Like what books I read, which books I like, what I want to be. You know me", I say and he shakes his head.

"Those are standard stuff. I don't know why you don't eat", he says and my mind automatically goes to panic mode. I look out the window, tapping my fingers against the cold window.

"Rory?", he asks and I shut him out. Why did he have to mention that? "Rory?", he says again and I turn to him.

"I'm sorry I'm such a burden to you", I meant for my voice to be strong but it cracks at the end.

"What? You're not", he says softly and I pick at my nails.

"You have to feed me, you have to drive me, heck you even have to talk for me", I say and he looks at me like I'm talking nonsense.

"Rory, I do those things because I want to. I would like to help you. The driving was an agreement for you to fake dating me. And I talk for you because I know it makes it easier on you, I'm sorry if it seemed like I did everything for you", he says in a breath and I blow out a breath.

"I feel bad", I admit and he blows out a raspberry.

"Don't. I'm happy to help you, Rory. I do everything knowing that I don't need anything from you. But I would like to know more about you", he says, meeting my eyes.

"Why?", I ask.

"I like you", he says and then glances around like he didn't mean to tell me that. I feel my heart beat faster at the confirmation of my earlier assumptions-- Assumptions I wanted to be wrong about.

Chapter Ten

A urora

"You can't", I say to him.

"Why not?", he asks me and I close my eyes. All of my memories come to me and in an instant, I'm crying.

"I have a ton of shit. I have a lot of trust issues. And I can't, well, I won't let you touch me. Why would you want to go through that?", I ask.

"Rory, I can live without touching you. I would like to, but if you can't have me do that, then I won't. I don't need a relationship being built on physical touch anyway", he says like the words came right out of me, what I wanted him to say.

He continues,"As for your personal issues, I want to know about them. I want to help you through them." Oliver cannot be the same guy who approached me the first day, yes, he was nice but this is next level.

"Because you like me?", I say and he nods.

"I don't know", I say and he looks at me to keep talking. "I'm not sure if I like you."

"Sure you do", he says and I let out a laugh at his cockiness.

"I'm not sure if I would like to admit liking you. I'm scared."

"Of?", he persists and I take a breath.

"I'm scared of not knowing. Not knowing when you would no longer want me, or when you would want more and I won't be able to provide that for you. I'm scared of being attached to you and putting a lot of pressure on you", I say with a tear sliding down my cheek.

"That's a fear that you would never overcome without living through it. You have to trust me in order for those things to not happen. And Rory", he starts but then stops.

"Yeah?"

He lets out an embarrassed laugh, long and breathy, "It's been only a month and I'm already attached to you. So whether you like me or not it will not deteriorate my attachment to you."

I start to laugh because all of this is crazy. A boy liking me? A boy wanting to fight to be with me? A boy not running away when I tell him that I can't provide for him what he might want? It's all crazy. I reach out my hand and put it in his and then pull it to my lap.

"You're crazy", I admit to him and he only grins at me.

"You like me", I tell him to which he nods at as well.

"Well", I say, closing my eyes, "I like you too." I open my eyes to find that he is looking at me with a lot of intensity than before. His eyes flit down to my lips and I feel myself leaning away from him. Is he about to kiss me? I squeeze his hand and say, "But can we maybe table this conversation. I'm not ready."

"Sure", he says and I let another tear slip at his kindness. I'm not sure of how I would react if I was in his position; definetly not in the way he is.

"Oliver?", I say to him in the darkness of his car and he hums.

"I won't have you waiting forever for me okay?"

"I'm not worried about that."

"I promise to share more about me to you and hopefully I can work through my trust issues with you", I say and he hums again.

"Stop humming", I say to him and he jerks his head to me. His eyes meet my face and a slow smile appears on his face, "Sorry."

"Are you entirely okay with this?", I asked him.

"Yes, Rory. I'm waiting for you whenever you're ready. In the meantime, you promise to make more of an effort with me?"

"Yes", I say and we spend a few more minutes in silence before he pulls out of his driveway and toward my house.

□•□•□••

Ever since the whole confession, I have started to feel more comfortable around Oliver. He has shown to be trusting so why should I not trust him? And honestly, I'm so tired of caging myself away from the world and not enjoying moments because I have things to deal with at home. That being said, I have started to share my childhood stories with Oliver.

"No, trust me. Frankie really liked this older guy the year she was fourteen and she really wanted his number, and I had dared her. So she ran down the hill in an attempt to follow him but instead she fell and rolled past him. And get this, she was so determined that she waited until he came all the way down the hill, she asked him his number", I say trying not to laugh in order for him to hear me.

"Did she get his number?", he asks and I shake my head.

"He was 21, visiting Italy to celebrate it. He said no but Frankie had the biggest smile on her face when I reached her. She had placed a hand on her hip and said 'and that's how it's done, rory' and I hadn't been more proud of my sister in that moment."

"She sounds like a good sister. Are you guys still close?", he asks and I play with the edge of the table, suddenly wanting to not speak anymore. But I do, I had made a promise to make more of an effort with him.

"She hasn't called me back ever since she moved to Italy for college", I say and Oliver frowns. I shrug,"We have a plan though. Both of us are going to head there for college so she is just waiting for me."

"Rory?"

"Yeah?", I say tucking a peice of hair behind my ear. I turn to see him looking at me with pity in his eyes.

"You know that's bullshit?", he says and I shake my head.

"We had a plan. We talked about this", I say and he frowns deeper. His hand on mine tighten and he gives me an encouraging look.

"She wouldn't back out of the plan", I say softly, more to myself and he nods. "She wouldn't abandon me." This time I had whispered it.

"But she is already", he says and I start to pull my hand away from his. My head hurts, my heart is heavy. She wouldn't back out of the plan, she promised me. Oliver pulls me back and says,"I'm sorry, Rory."

"She wouldn't back out of the plan", I say softly again and he only runs a hand down my palm. I take a deep breath in and repeat it like a mantra over and over again.

"Frankie was my best friend", I admit to him. "When life got hard she would sneak into my room and the both of us would watch cheesy movies that are set in Italy."

"That sounds nice", he says and I nod.

"She will call me as soon as I am done with highschool and everything will be okay", I say and Oliver nods.

"Everything will be perfectly fine", he says and then the bell rings for us to leave lunch. We both stand up and Oliver walks me to my class.

"Frankie is still my best friend, right?", I ask him and he nods.

"And if she is not. I will be. I'll be here for you", he says and I smile up at him. With a final squeeze of my hand, he pulls away and starts heading to his own class.

□•□•□•□•

"I have a party this week that the both of us have to attend", he says to me the next week on the way to school. I frown and look at him, his hair has gotten longer but it still suits his face.

"I don't want to go", I say and he sighs.

"I know that", he starts,"But a girl invited me and then she started flirting with me so I mentioned that you would be there with me." I try not to feel anything at the fact that another girl is filtering with me. If it wasn't for the confession, I would be wondering why he didn't just choose one of them. Why he chose me. But now that I know what he told me, I feel envious of the other girls.

I wonder how it would be to turn him on? He certainly isn't turned on for a girl who cannot go a day without crying.

I cross my arms over my chest and say,"You're fault for being good looking." Oliver let out a laugh so loud I had to cover my ear, and his laugh continued as he kept driving. After a good five minutes, he turned to me and jutted out his jaw,"You think I'm good looking?" If it wasn't for the driving, he would definitely have crossed his arms.

"You know you are. The girls all fawn over you for that reason, you think they care about basketball. Only a handful do", I say and he laughs again and places a mock hand on his heart.

I chuckle and say,"You think girls are fawning over Jake?" Jake is a guy on his team and he is so short, he almost compares to me. He also isn't that good looking. Oliver laughs on and on again and I join in on the laugh, leaning more toward him.

"I didn't know you didn't like Jake", he says and I shrug. "He keeps staring at me. At us. Come to think of it maybe he has a slight crush on you."

"No way", he says and laughs once more before stopping abruptly and saying,"Does he?"

"Chi lo sa", I say, letting the Italian fall on my tongue. Who knows? He glances at me and I repeat it in English.

"Back to the topic at hand, will you please come to the party with me?", he asks, his hand searching for my own and grabbing a hold of it. I groans again and say,"I don't even know what to wear."

"Just a fancy top and regular jeans", he says and I shake my head.

"I'd like to keep my hoodie on", I say and he shakes his head.

"Party, Rory. So ditch the hoodie", he says and I make a point of jutting out my bottom lip and pouting.

"I love my hoodie", I say and he laughs.

"I know you do, but ditch it", he says and I shake my head.

"You owe me."

"What would you like, princesa?", he says and I groan at his wrong translation.

"Principessa", I correct,"A book. And two if you make me take off my hoodie."

"Consider it done", he says and I huff.

"Odio le ragazze gelose", I murmur and Oliver laughs despite not knowing what it means but I guess my tone and body language gave it away.

I hate jealous girls.

I slump back into my seat and cross my hands over my chest. He glances at me and says,"It'll be fun."

"Sure", I say low and look out the window. I definitely wasn't ready for this party, I knew it might've come with the agreement of being his fake girlfriend but I still wasn't prepared for it.

Author's Note: Hiii. My first time popping up here, so from the next chapter (Oliver's POV) things start to move fast. Some may love it, others may not. But I promise that I have a few good plans ahead of us. Thank you for taking the time out of your day to read my book.

I appreciate it, so much more than you can know. I've written a few and this is the first I'm sharing, so.... I appreciate it a lot.

Bye, see you guys next time!!!

Chapter Eleven

O liver

This week we don't win the game which I try not to feel too bombed out about. I think about the party that Aurora is accompanying me on. She gave me permission to use her full name after I put up a fight earlier this week.

I remember the way she looked at me when I said "Your name is too pretty to be discarded". She looked happy and after trying out her name on my tongue a few times, she gave in.

Aurora

Too pretty.

I'm waiting for her as she heads into the bathroom to change into her party outfit. I'm not sure what I am expecting from her but when she returns in a baby pink corset top I try not to stare at her. The sleeve is basically not there as it is so thin and I try not to look at the small inch of skin showing on her stomach. I let out a low whistle at the sight of her, obviously failing on my attempts to not stare at her, and she hugs her body with her arm.

I wonder how it would feel for me to hug her instead. She sighs and walks past me. "You owe me three books."

I catch up with her,"I thought it was two." I don't really care about how many I'm buying her, I just want to make conversation.

She looks back at me and her gorgeous hair falls down her back,"It was. But I had to go out and buy this shirt, so..."

"Right", I say, trying not to ogle it like I did before. It just makes her look so much prettier if that was even possible. She stops by my car and I open the door up for her. She gets in and I follow suit. Twenty minutes later, we are at the party and Aurora has yet to stop complaining.

"Come on, try to have a little fun", I tell her as we walk through the front door. The music is so loud I can hardly hear properly and there are so many people that my hands immediately search for hers. She has made it seem okay that I can hold her hand first and I've been using it to my advantage. I walk through the house and to the kitchen where it is quieter.

A few girls are wandering about and when they see Aurora they stop in front of her. I watch as they compliment her, her shirt, her hair, her makeup and Aurora modestly smiles at them.

"Thank you", she says and the girls look up at me.

"You have everything huh", one of the girls with red hair says but not unkindly.

"Oh Oliver. Yeah", Aurora says and the girls giggle. She giggles along with them and I feel a sense of pride.

"Well come find us if you want to chat", the other girl says and Aurora nods. The three of them leave and I watch her turn back to me with a smile on her face.

"They liked me", she tells me and I laugh.

"Of course, you are kind and stunning", I say automatically and I watch as her face changes color. She giggles and then grabs a water off of the table.

"Are you going to drink?" She asks and the tone of her voice makes me think she might not want me to.

"Do you want me to drink?", I ask her and she shakes her head.

"I mean you are the driver and I can't drive but if you want to, you can. But—"

"I won't drink. Come on let's find a Gatorade", I say and walk around the counter. I find a blue one and take a sip from it before capping it up and placing it in my pocket. We walk out of the kitchen and into the living room where there are so many people it is hard to move through.

The music gets louder so I turn us around and head to the back of the house, past the kitchen. I hear Austin's voice and head out the back patio. I find him sitting on one of the patio chairs with a lot of people sorrounding him. When he sees me, he stands up and heads to us.

"My favorite man is here" he says loud enough for everyone to look for me. The eyes are nothing new for me but they are for Aurora who is trying to hide behind me. I squeeze her hand and let go if it so I can hug my friend.

"Is that Rory?", Austin asks to let go of me and surprised by her choice of clothing. I let him hype her up for a few seconds before shutting him up by slapping his shoulder. He laughs and then whispers,"She looks so pretty."

"I know", I whisper back and he moves on to the crowd surrounding us. He takes a seat back on his spot and points to on beside him. Singular seat. He only raises an eyebrow and I whisper to Aurora,"You'll have to sit on my lap."

"I can stand", she says and I look around at the people watching us.

"I won't touch you", I say softly and she also glances at all the people and manages a nod. I feel nervous as I take a seat on he patio chair and point to one of my leg for her to take a seat. I watch as she picks at her fingernails while taking a seat on me. Automatically, I feel warmth go through me at the aspect of her being so close and touching me. I take a deep breath in and reach for my Gatorade prompting her to shreik inaudibly and putting a hand on my neck. I feel my spine straighten up at her touch, her hand so soft and delicate.

"This okay?", she whispers in my ear and I nod.

"If it's okay with you", I say back to her. She nods, tightening her hold on me and I feel myself get clammy. She only stares at me with uncertainty so I look away from her.

"What are we doing?" I ask the group instead.

"Playing thruth or dare", Austin says and I groan. We play this game at almost every party and it gets kind of boring.

"I've never played this game" , her sweet voice whispers in my ear and I turn to her. She plays with the hair at the end of my hair. I find my voice and say,"Do you want to?"

She chews on her bottom lip and then nods. "Then we'll play", I say to her loud enough for the group to hear. "You first, Austin. Go get a girl's number."

A couple of girls in this sorrounding group pipe up with their phones but I chuckle, "Not someone from here."

Austin stands up, puts a hand on his heart and says, "Sorry girls." He leaves as they groan and I laugh. Jake pipes up and says, "While he is doing that, Oliver's girlfriend, truth or dare?"

"Her name is Rory", I pitch in annoyed at his words, he knew her name. I hear Aurora thinking beside me and she looks at me for help. I only keep her eye contact and so she releases a breath and says, "Truth."

Jake groans in disappoint and I feel her scoot closer to me. He thinks for a second before saying, "What is your happy place?" Aurora takes a deep breath in my ear and then takes her time thinking. She finds the answer, and I watch as she tries it out on her mouth silently.

After she is ready she answers, "Italy with my mom and older sister." I frown at the answer knowing that the probability of this happening again is low, maybe her sister but her mom is not coming back.

Jake smiles at the answer and then points to me. I groan and he laughs. "Make out with Rory for a minute straight." I'm about to open my mouth to object but Austin comes back with a whoop.

"I got her number!", he shouts and the crowd cheers. The girl on my lap sits up and when I look at her she has a small smile on her face. He liked his dare, liked the energy he brought with him.

"So who is next?" Austin asks taking his seat.

"Jake dared me to kiss Aurora for a minute", I say rolling my eyes but Austins eyebrows raise up in eagerness.

"That sounds hot", he says and the crowd agrees with him. I look at Aurora who is already looking at me.

"Do we have to?", she whispers.

"I usually never back down a dare, but if you don't want to, we can just leave", I say to her trying to maintain eye contact. She looks back at the crowd and then at me, her eyes flitting to my lips. She draws her bottom lip in her mouth and her eyes meet mine. My heart beats in my chest at the way she is looking at me. Something makes her nod and lean up to me.

I lean down and meet her in the middle pressing my lips gently against hers. I almost let out a gasp at her soft lips and how it feels good against mine. I let go to look at her and the crowd boos. I ignore them and put out my index finger signaling for them to give us a moment. Aurora puts a finger to her lips and looks up at me. Did she like it? I'm about to open my mouth to ask when she smiles letting go of the finger.

"Can I put my hand on your jaw?", I ask her and she looks down at my hand on my lap, away from her.

"Why?", she asks and I chuckle.

"You'll see", I whisper to her and she nods slowly. I take a breath in and my hand goes under her jaw softly. Her breath hitches at my touch but she only leans closer to me, her hand steady behind my head. I put my mouth against hers gain and use my hand on her jaw to move her closer. I kiss her gently, letting her get comfortable with me, and only kiss her with more power when I feel her slipping past me. She makes a noise when I run my tongue on her bottom lip, demanding access. She opens her mouth and I'm about to slip it in when the crowd cheers loudly.

"That's enough", I hear the sound of my best friends voice pulls me away from Aurora with a bite on her bottom lip. She gasps as she lets go and drops her hand from me. I gently take my hand off her jaw and watch as she puts a hand on her lips, sensing the tingling like I am right now. I run my tongue along my lip, tasting her lips. She tasted sweet; I want to kiss her again but she looks down at her lap and I can see her hand shaking.

"Are you okay?", I whisper to her. She looks up at me and shrugs,"I don't know what to say."

"Say the word and I'll kiss you again. But until then I'll let this play in my mind in it's place", I say to her, bold.

She looks at me with what seems like amusement and says,"Okay." I flash her a grin and turn back to the crowd who has already moved on to dare a guy on the team to walk around and take a sip of ten people's drink. The rest of the game, I watch as Aurora watches with a small smile on her face, sitting up when she finds one interesting. I try to stop my racing heart at her every move even though she doesn't make an effort to touch me again but it doesn't seem to work.

She has made her way into my heart and I don't want to let her go. The thought makes me smile.

Chapter Twelve

A urora

The party finished a good hour ago, but Oliver had taken us to a drive thru instead of my house. We ordered food and talked in an empty parking lot for ten minutes. Oliver has been in a good mood and I have been in a talkative mood. I've been sharing more stories of my childhood and Oliver has been attentively listening.

"I miss Italy", I tell him, shoving a fry in my mouth.

"When was the last time you went?", he asks pulling out of the driveway once he realizes it's past midnight.

"The summer before my mom died."

"Why doesn't your father take you?", he asks me casually reaching for my fries. I swat his hand away and he grins at me.

"He doesn't see a point in going where his family is not", I say nervewrecked at the fact that I'm speaking to him about my dad. I've been not wanting to go home tonight knowing that he will be there and will probably hurt me. Probably is putting it lightly the only way I would avoid him is if he had already passed out from drinking.

"Well, you should visit this summer", he says.

I take a sip of his coke regretting that I ordered water,"Maybe." I take a bigger sip of his coke and then hold it up to his mouth. He glances down at it and takes a sip.

"Take a good one because I'm stealing the rest", I tell him and he chuckles pushing the cup away, toward me. There is a lightness in his demeanor at the fact that I'm eating.

"All yours", he smiles at me.

I clutch the drink to my chest,"Thank you." Unsurprisingly, I had put my jacket back on as soon as we got in the car. He pulls into my driveway a few minutes later and I feel my heart become heavy at the sight of my house. I find that the living room light is on, and a shiver runs through me despite being in a heated car. I turn to him, willing him to share a story so I can stay out here longer.

"I liked your energy tonight", he compliments and I beam at him. The compliment makes me feel a little more confident.

I tuck in a hair behind my ear,"It was a fun night."

"Really?", he asks leaning toward me,"What was your favorite part?" The look in his eyes lets me know that he is wanting me to talk about the kiss.

The kiss

My first kiss was in front of a whole crowd and yet I felt like it was just the two of us. He had been so gentle with me but a little more harsh, dominant, at the second one. But the first kiss was so gentle and so good. I close my eye to remember it and it comes back to me so vivid that I open my eye quickly.

"Um I liked the truth or dare", I manage to say and his eyes shine even in the dark of only the streetlights illuminating light.

"What part?", he says softy and I feel my heart flutter at his words. Something pools at the bottom of my stomach and I suddenly feel like I can fly. I lean closer to him and before I can think twice about it, I plant a kiss on his cheek. It's a quick one but it warms my whole body like we had been kissing for hours.

"That", I whisper softly against his cheek and then lean away from him. He blinks a few times and leans forward again but I open the door and say,"I'm leaving."

"Aurora", my name is a soft whisper on his tongue and I close my eyes to remember it. I love my name when he says it, and only when he says it. He is always soft and gentle with it, like my name is of a delicate thing.

"Yeah?", I say, opening my eyes.

"Have a good weekend, yeah?", he says in a whisper and I nod. He runs a hand through his hair and says,"I'll see you later, then."

"Until then", I say and close the door. I walk past his jeep and toward my house, where the sight of it makes me shudder. I close my eye and before I can think twice of it, I turn around and walk right back to his truck. I find him looking at me from the driver's seat and without saying a word, I reach for him. But of course, I can't wrap an arm around him, I only place my hand in his.

"Dammi la forza", I whisper to him. Give me strength. He only squeezes my hand and I look at him, wanting him to take me to his house. To not let me go inside to a monster I have to face everyday. I want him to wrap his arms around me and shelter me from the world. To be there for me.

"Good Night, Oli", I whisper to him instead and he lets go of my hand.

"Night", he says grinning at me. I wrap my hands around me and take myself back to my house. I hear his car drive away and close my eyes at what is coming. It is close to one a.m right now so I can't imagine this would be good.

□•□•□•□

"What were you doing out with him all night?", he shouts at me from the living room as soon as I walk in and I tell myself to walk faster and up the stairs. I make a point to leave but his hand on my hair yanks me back and I groan at the excruciating pain. "Are you whoring around?"

This sentence doesn't surprise me, what he adds to it makes my blood boil a hundred degrees over.

"...like that mother of yours", he spits in my face and I ball my fists up.

"She was not!", I shout and he laughs so hard and so loud it makes my stomach lurch in disgust.

He lets go of my hair and instead pulls at the hoodie I'm wearing, pulls the zipper down. "Your mother went to Italy every summer, what do you think she was doing?"

I try to pull my hoodie back over me but he yanks it off of me and bares his teeth when he sees what I am wearing. "You're giving that guy a display of your body? Letting him do whatever he wants with you?

"I am not", I shout back but he only pulls at my waist tighter and when I try to pull away, he yanks me back. I close my eye and feel his hand snake around my neck. My throat closes up and I'm about to slip away from consious when his other hand comes up to my mouth and he tries to slip a finger in my mouth.

I feel sick.

"Open up", he whispers his mouth hot against my face but I clam my mouth shut. I can't do this. When I don't, his hand instead makes contact with my face and the sharp sound makes me open my eye. I don't feel the sting on my face though, I've become immune to it. His hand tightens around my neck once more and he continues his tangent,"Your mother went to Italy to hook with guys. Younger guys.

She showed off her body. She captured the attention of young guys. And what do you think happened every night?"

"No", I slip the word out of my mouth and he laughs.

"She slept with them. Let them do whatever they wanted. She fed off of that."

"You're lying", I say and he pushes me back so hard I fall on the floor. My body makes contact with the ground and he walks over me,"And you are talking so much. What happned yo the rat who never spoke huh? That boy teaches you to say unnecessary things."

I ignore him and try to get off the floor but he steps on one of my hand. A sharp pain goes through me and he laughs once more. "You are pathetic. Nobody wants you here, God your sister left to never come back because of you."

"Frankie loved me", I whisper and his laugh gets louder.

"Then where is she?"

"She is--- ", my words falter when I realize I don't know what to say. He laughs and kicks a leg to my exposed skin of my torso. I grunt in pain and he fiends off that as he kicks me again. I roll to my side in an attempt to stop him but he only laughs harder and kicks me once more. My stomach lurches and I close my mouth only for it to open forcefully when he kicks me once more and I throw up. I look at the floor around me at the mixture of throw up and blood.

Oh God.

"Stop", I whisper but he only leans down and gets a hold on my hair. He pulls me up with it and says,"What was that?"

"Stop", I say again but he looks away and when he looks back at me for a second I see the kind father he used to be. He would stand outside on the porch everytime we came home from school just to hug us. He would tuck me into bed after reading me a story even though I would ask him to reread it a million times, but he would read it as many times as I asked, with even a small smile on his face. He would pack my suitcase for me the night before I left for Italy even though my mom had yelled at me countless times for leaving it for last minute. He was gentle, he was kind, he was everything Frankie and I could've imagined.

But that lasted for a second as his eyes darkened and he slammed my head on the floor. I didn't even have a moment to react to it as he did it continuously. So many times, back and forth. I threw up again only this time it was just blood.

Back and forth.

Until I passed out.

□•□•□•□

Author's Note:and so it begins, my friends.

Chapter Thirteen

Aurora

The next time I wake up, the sun blinds me. I rub a hand at my eye but it worsens the pain in my head. It smells horrible, I take notice and when I look to my side I find vomit. Was it mine? I couldn't tell. I tried to sit up but my head weighed a ton. So much. I placed my hand on the back of head and came up with a red splotches. It is still wet, how is it still wet.

Not that wet, just a tiny bit wet. Enough to scare me. I groan as I use as much strength as I can muster to sit up. I do, but my head falls off to the side. Oh God. I look around at the ripped up hoodie of mine and the door that is left slightly ajar, cold air sipping into the house.

The events of last night come back to me so vividly that I hold my stomach and throw up again.

I need to leave.

My ribs hurt and when I try to stand up, I fail and fall back down the floor. Where is my phone? I search for it in my pockets but do not find it. I look to the ripped up hoodie and it's not anywhere there. I look toward my throw up and find that it fell somewhere under the table. I take a deep breath in and crawl to my phone. It takes a long time to get to it, but when I do, I want to smile.

Only I don't, it hurts to.

I find that it has more cracks now and when I open it, there is only 5 percent battery. I look through my contacts before realizing I should call the police. But what would they do? They would ask me too many questions right now and I'm tired. So freaking tired. With shaky fingers I look through to find Frankie's name. When I press on it it goes automatically to voicemail, which shouldn't be much of a surpsise to me but right now it hits hard. I close my eye and his words from last night come back to me.

Then where is she?

A tear falls on the phone and I wipe at it. Oliver's name shines and I feel my heart flutter at it. He can help me. I press on his phone and it keeps ringing. I look at the time to see that it is six o'clock on a Saturday. He is my only hope so I keep ringing him, until finally he answers on the third try.

"Miss me already?", he says, his voice barely audible, and I let out a sob at the happiness in hearing his voice. "Aurora?", his voice is much more sharper now as opposed to the tired one from before.

"I need you", only three words. I can only manage to say those three words.

"Are you home?", he asks and I let out a bigger sob.

Home. The word has lost it's meaning.

"I need you", I repeat once more and hear a bed creak on his phone line.

"Stay with me. I'll be here in ten minutes", he says and I fists the phone in my hand. I listen to his rushed breathing and in a minute I hear key jingling and a door shutting behind him. He is coming, I repeat to myself over and over again. After what seems like forever I hear the cut off of an engine and another door shut. I look up to hear footsteps on my front porch and a knock on the door before it creaks open further.

"Aurora?", I hear his voice and want to jump into his arms but can't. My body has shut down on the floor and I hate to admit it but I had laid down next to my own vomit again. I look to see him rush past my ripped hoodie and toward me. He doesn't even react to the smell of the room, only crouches down next to me. His eyes are wild and frantic, searching for the hurt on my face.

"What happened?", he asks and tries searching for the source, his eyes scanning the open living area.

"Get me out of here", I say to him and place a hand on his knee. He looks down at my body and at my face before a frown settles on his face. I reach up and poke his cheek close to his mouth where the dimple would have been.

"Dimple", I say and his eyebrows furrowed in confusion. I only poke the spot harder and say,"You should smile more." He gives me a soft smile before moving on, but my mind replays the smile over and over again.

"Can you move?", he tells me and I shake my head, barely. I can't get it to move.

"Well, I'm about to carry you. Is that okay?", he whispers and I move my hand to his neck, gripping it.

"Please", the word comes out a mess but he understands it and places a hand under my waist. "My head", I say to him and he places a gentle hand underneath my head and it hurts. It hurts so much as he picks me up and walks me out of my house. I look up at his eyes, eyes full of worry and it makes me frown. He takes me outside where the clouds look back at me and I reach up to touch them. They are beautful.

He opens up the car door and places me in it. He let's me go and I pull at his arm,"Don't go."

"I'm not going anywhere", he says and reaches up and pulls down the seatbelt over my torso. It hurts, my ribs. He sees the pain in my face and loosens it for me. I give him a smile, well attempt to and he closes the door softly. I follow him as he walks to the other side of the door, his steps rushed.

"No hospitals", I say to him when he gets in the car. He glances at me and then at my body. "Please", I add and he nods.

"My dad's a doctor, he will help you", he says as he starts driving.

"At the hospital?", I whisper and he shakes his head.

"My house", he says and I let out another sob. I don't stop crying as he drives the short distance to his house. When he pulls into his driveway, I hear a couple of worried voices and look out to see his parents rushing out of the house in their pajamas. It makes me glance over at him to find that he is also in his pajama pants and a white shirt, well pressed so it tells me that he put it on right before walking out of his house.

"Rory?", his mom shouts when she opens my door and I notice the tears in her eyes. I must look like a mess. She puts a hand on her mouth and Oliver rushes past her and toward me. He places his hand under my waist and one on my head as he pulls me out and carries me to his house.

"Dad, your kit", he shouts at his father as we head into his house. He drops me off gently on the couch but I don't let go of my hand on his neck.

"Stay with me?", I whisper to him and he nods. I move my hand toward his arm and wrap it around it. He feels warm. His father emerges in a white uniform and a box of tools in his hand and I cower away at him.

"Its just my dad", Oliver whispers to me but I still hide beside him. His mother comes up to my other side and I watch as she silently cries. "Don't cry, Victoria. I'm going to be okay."

"How do you know that?", she asks me and Oliver shoots his mother a look. I look up at his face, his handsome, kind face and say,"He took me away from the monster."

And then I pass out again.

□•□□•□•□•

The next time I wake up, my head hurts less and my body is on a more comfortable surface. I turn my head to find Oliver sitting beside me with a hand in my hair. I bet it stinks, I want to tell him. But I can't find my voice. I stir to the side to find his parents in the dining room, talking. I sit up and Oliver places a hand on the back of my hair to help me.

"How are you feeling, sweetheart?", he asks me and I continue staring at him. He is still here, like he promised he would be. I scoot closer to him, but it's not enough, so I climb into his lap and bury my face in his chest. I feel his body stiffen before he relaxes it fully and his arms wrap around my shoulders. My entire body relaxes at his touch and I let out another sob. How can he feel so good. His hug is exactly want I needed so I move even closer to him and look up at him.

He smiles down at me and says,"Better?" I place a hand around his neck and nod. He doesn't say anything more as I bury my face in his neck to create warmth. I'm cold, I realize. We stay in this postion for so long I'm afraid his legs are asleep underneath me. His parents walk into the room and I look at them. I can't get myself to look at his father but I send a smile to his mother.

I look at Oliver and sniff,"I think I need a shower."

"The bandages on your head is waterproof but you should be careful with it", his father says from somewhere behind me. I tighten my hold on Oliver and ask,"Can I take a shower?"

"Of course", it's his mother who answers and Oliver only nods. I reach up and place a kiss on his cheek. "Maybe you should shower also."

"Oh wow", he laughs soflty but carries the both us off the couch. "You can shower in my room and I'll shower in my parents. Come on." I take his hand and together the both of us slowly walk up the stairs and toward his room.

My body craves for the warm water and to ease any memory of my father's hand on me. I no longer believe that my father could change. He had a chance yesterday but he ruined it. I try not to cry thinking about it. Oliver gives my hand a squeeze and I muster the courage to face the rest of the day.

Chapter Fourteen

O liver

My mind has been clouded by the thoughts of Aurora as soon as I heard her sob on the phone. It sounded inhuman and so raw; it made me jump out of bed. I should've known something would happen to her when she walked back around and clung to me. She had shuttered at the sight of her house, but I had only focused on the fact that she had warmed up to me.

I feel stupid. I felt stupid as I walked in her house and saw her laying helplessly on the floor, a pool of blood under her head. I felt helpless as well, and I felt my heart break at the sight of it. Aurora is strong, I knew that, but in that moment I saw how vulnerable she could be.

I need you, she had admitted to be on the phone; begged. Aurora never begs so I had ran out of my house in the clothes I wear to bed. When I asked to carry her, her voice broke at the word please and I felt my heart clench again at her vulnerability.

Somebody hurt her, I had thought the whole time she was sobbing in the car. I had been clenching the steering wheel telling myself that I would get justice for her. Somebody used her vulnerability to hurt her. Hurt her so bad she passed out. Hurt her so bad she became delirious.

Dimple. You should smile more, she had said in her state of delirium and I had never wanted to hug her close to my chest more than before. My heart had clenched when she climbed into my lap and buried herself in my chest. She clung to me as her safety net and I would never let her go.

After my quick shower, upon her recommendation, I walked in my room and grabbed two change of clothes. One set for me and the other for her. I set the clothes on my bed and went back to my parents bathroom to change into mine. After I was fully dressed and ready for the day, I walked downstairs to eat.

It's already 12 o'clock which means that Aurora had passed out by me on the couch for close to three hours. I've never seen someone so unsettled when sleeping. She had tossed and turned the whole time and the only thing that helped was me playing with her hair; she had calmed down then, not by much though.

I walk into the kitchen to find my dad sitting at the table. Aurora was afraid of my dad, that much I gathered. Did she assume he was going to hurt her? My dad would never. The last time I got punished physically was before I was five. But still, she cowered away from him and toward me.

He is sipping on coffee as I grab myself some. I take a seat beside him and he looks up at me then. He tosses his phone aside and looks around me. "Rory not done yet?"

"No, she's probably enjoying the warm water", I say.

My dad looks at me, his eyes soft, and says,"Is she scared of me?" I run a hand through my hair, I knew my dad would catch on but this quick?

I nod and my dad frowns. I put my hand out,"No, she was afraid of me at first too. She wouldn't even let me help her walk when she sprained her ankle, not even let me help her up when she fell."

"Really?", he says wanting to hear more.

I sigh,"It's not my story to tell, but Aurora has always been afraid of anyone's touch."

My dad smiles softly,"She's not afraid of your touch anymore. In fact, she prefers it." I feel myself blushing and my dad laughs, waving his hand in the air. "I just mean in the way she moved away from me to you and in the way your mom and I found her fully on your lap earlier this morning."

That moment had been so raw that I didn't even have the time to be embarrassed at the affection been shown in front of my parents. I run another hand through my hair,"Yeah, she warmed up to me."

"That's good. But you need to be careful to not deteriorate her trust", he says and I nod.

"I'd never do anything she wouldn't want me to. Heck, I wanted to hug her more times than I'd like to admit and I held myself back. She's special and I recognize that", I say. I felt nervous saying that so I had looked down at my hand but when I look up at my dad, I find his eyes elsewhere. I follow his sight and turn around to find Aurora standing beside me.

My dad puts a hand to his chest,"Ask Nolan if you need anything, I left some cream for your ribs on the table."

Aurora looks down at the floor and nods. "Thank you, Mr. Baker", she says despite her unintended fear of my father.

"You're welcome, honey", my dad says and then grabs his mug and stands up from the table. "I'll leave you two down here. Nolan, your mother made brunch for the both of you. Rory, get some food in you, okay?" Aurora nods and I wave goodbye to my father who winks at me as he leaves. It dawns on me that Aurora heard what I said and it makes a blush appear on my cheek.

She pulls up the sweatpants she is wearing of mine with her lips parted in awe. "I'll get you a safety pin", I say to her but she only folds it down a few times before taking a seat at the table and I notice that it is the one closest to me. Something about the tiny detail makes me smile.

"I heard what you said", she starts and I look away to fight the urge to blush again but she continues,"Thank you." Her words surprise me and I look at her. She looks exhausted still, her face clean but red. The hoodie is bigger on her than usual and her hair is wet past her shoulders. I wish I could hug her again.

She places a hand on the table and brings it toward mine. I watch as she places it on top if mine and looks up at me with a little smile that is more of a grimace. My heart hurts for her. "Thank you for rescuing me today. And I promise I will share my story with you, but I'm afraid if I do right now, I'd break down, and I've wasted enough tears today."

I give her hand a squeeze and say,"Take your time. As much as you need. We are all here to help you not demand answers from you."

"Thank you", she says again and I nod at her.

"I'll get you some food. No, get us some food", I say and she nods letting go of my hand. I stand up from the table and walk to the counter to find that my mom made waffles that are still warm. I grab the huge stack and the eggs next to it.

I set it down on the table and Aurora pales at the sight of it. My heart clenches again but I manage to move forward and grab us two glasses of water. I set it down on the table and sat down as well. I hand her some waffles and set the syrup next to her.

"I don't think I can stomach this", she says and I frown. "Do you guys have some fruits? That sounds good right now."

"Of course", I say and stand up and walk to the counter where I spot the fruit bowl. I grab the whole thing and set it on the table. She stares at it for a minute before grabbing a banana. I look away from her and grab some waffles for myself. I start eating.

"So, where's your mom?", the girl next to me asks and I have to think about it.

"I know she doesnt have work wait", I say and with the both of us quiet I hear talking from upstairs. "Up there with my dad", I say and she nods.

"Oliver", she starts and then looks away. I give her time to speak and when she does she sounds nervous. "Your parents....are they okay with me staying here today?"

"What, are you kidding?", I say,"Considering what I saw at your home, you're not ever going back ."

She chews on her bottom lip,"But are they okay with it?"

"I'm sure my mom is clearing out the guest room as we speak."

"la gentilezza è sottovalutata", she murmurs and I lean closer to her to hear her better. She grabs my hand and says,"Kindness is underrated."

"Oh", I say and then try out the italian phrase under my tongue but it doesn't work out.

"Bel ragazzo", she says to me and when I open my mouth to answer she leans in and plants a kiss on my cheek. I feel my whole body stiffen and she moves toward my ear. "Handsome boy."

The compliment makes my cheeks warm and she laughs pulling away from me. "And he blushes", she says incredulously and I feel myself blush harder. I'm about to tease her back but she makes a move of picking up some eggs so I let her. She needs the energy the food would provide her.

"You're strong", I say to her once the both of us are done with the food. "And I'm so sorry that happened to you."

"Thank you, Oli", she whispers and I give her hand, that she slipped into mine, a squeeze.

□□•□•□•□•

It takes us a couple of hours and two movies later to get out of the couch. I had booted up some disney movie on the tv and Aurora had sat next to me watching the screen. I didn't say anything when she silently cried at a couple of scenes that had a family in it. She doesn't have a family anymore, I had realized at that moment. I don't know anything but I do know that her family is a mess. She smiled a few times at the movie though and that made me happy. Mostly, she stayed silent by my side as I worked on a little bit of homework. My teachers compromised where I get a lot of weekend homework and only a little bit of weekday homework since I am a student athlete. It's the one rule I really appreciated.

After the ending of the second movie, I had gotten off of the couch to look at the clock. It's around 6 oclock and I really need to do a quick errand.

"What is it?", she says looking up at me and I glance at her and then at the door.

"I have to go run an errand."

"You're leaving?", she asks her expression worrisome. I put a hand on hers and ask,"Do you want to come with me?" Automatically she shakes her head.

"Do you have to go?", she asks and I nod. "So I'll have to stay alone at your house." She thinks to herself for a second and then looks up at me,"I'm scared."

"Don't be", I say quickly,"Go upstairs to my room. You'll be safe there." She thinks to herself for a long moment before nodding. I make a move to leave but she stops me by kneeling on the couch and placing her hands on my neck. I watch with a small smile on my face as she presses her body against mine in a hug. I replicate it by putting my hands around her waist. She takes a deep breath in and I follow her breathing technique.

She lets go of the hug, but I keep a loose hand on her waist. "Can you buy me a few things?"

"Sure, what do you need?", I ask her tightening my hold on her waist.

"I'm going to get my period tomorrow so I'll need some products and I need underwear", she says somewhat shy and I chuckle.

"I'll get them", I say and she smiles at me. Putting a hand under her chin, I say,"I'll see you later then, principessa." I memorized the nickname she taught me a while ago and seeing as it puts a smile on her face, I use it.

I lean in and press my cheek against hers, feeling her calmness on my skin, and pull away. I let go of her and start walking toward the front door, grab my keys, and when I look back, she is waving at me.

□•□•□

"Why are we going through the women's underwear section? Oh my God, are we buying lingerie for your girl?"Austin asks as soon as I walk into the women's section in Target. I picked out three books for her from the book section and now am searching for the things Aurora requested.

I glare at him,"No, ew. Aurora is staying over at my house for now and she needs some things."

"Your parents allowing her to stay?", he asks and I nod. He lets out a low whistle and I roll my eyes. Going through women's aisle is scandalous so I grab the first pack of underwear that seems to fit her I see. Austin glances down at it and then looks away from me.

"Why the hell are you blushing?", I ask him as we exist the aisle and he shakes his head. I ignore him and walk into the feminine aisle where I pick up a box of pads and tampons. Not sure which one she uses, but it would do. I also stop by the clothing section and walk through to find a cute matching set pajama. It is a blue set with tiny white flowers all over it and it is a long sleeve set so I get it. I purchase everything along with the things I need and walk out with a small victorious smile on my face.

"You're changing", Austin says when we get to the car and I raise an eyebrow at him.

"How so?", I ask.

"Simce when do you shop for those stuff?", he asks.

"Since Aurora requested for them", I say.

"But still. I used to watch you makeout with girls at parties and never call them back, its different with Aurora", he says and I glare at him.

"Rory to you", he gives me an incredulous look and I continue,"Aurora's different."

"That she is", he says,"I'm glad you're changing. I think it's a good thing."

"Me too", I say and look forward to see her at home.

Chapter Fifteen

A urora

Oliver had gotten me three books which I'm already in love with and also the other stuff I had asked for. He also got me a matching set of pajama which I changed to as soon as I could. When I showed him it, he asked for me to turn and it made me laugh. He only grinned at me with two thumbs up.

His parents made us go down for dinner shortly after he had came back and I tried to eat as much as I could. My appetite wasn't fully back but at least I ate more than I usually did. Oliver and I were about to head back upstairs when his mother stopped us by calling his name. His other name.

"Nolan, why don't you show Aurora to the guest room. I cleaned it out for her", she says looking at me and I nod at her.

"Thank you, Victoria", I say and she nods at me. The both of us head upstairs and Oliver walks us past his room toward the end of the hallway. He opens the door and we walk into the minimalist room, all white and clean. There is a queen sized bed and a nightstand. A dresser sits underneath a mirror and there are a few paintings on the wall.

"Hey look, at least these aren't your paintings", I joke with him and he laughs. I sit on the bed and then look at Oliver. It doesn't feel right being here. When I look at him I realize that it's because I'm going to be alone here. I didn't want to be alone.

"Can you stay?", I ask him and he glances at the door and then back at me. I tuck in a piece of hair behind my ear and say,"Not for the night. Just until after I fall asleep."

He scratches his head but then nods. I tuck myself into bed, pulling the blanket all the way up to my head. I watch Oliver stand there awkwardly in front of me and scoot over to give him space to lay down next to me.

"Just until I fall asleep", I murmur again and he obeys getting into bed beside me. He doesn't get into the blanket though and I try not to frown at that. I put a hand out of the blanket and tap his forehead. He looks at me and I feel myself smile. "Tell me your favorite memory."

"Before or after I met you?", he says softly and I smile harder. He chuckles and I shake my head,"Before."

And so he tells me the story of when he was first gifted a basketball at the age of four, I close my eye and listen as he tells me about how it felt in his hands, how truimpant he felt when he made his first basket. I'm imagining him growing up and learning more skills in the sport as his voice fades and my eyes close.

□•□•□•□

"I knew you would be back", his voice is far away and yet close. I open the door and walk in to find him sitting on the couch staring at me.

"Where's that boyfriend of yours?", he says with a smirk and I look back trying to find Oliver. He came with me, he should be here. But he is not.

I take a hesistant step back out of the house but not before he reaches me and yanks me back inside the house.

"You think you can leave me like your sister? Like your mother?", he shouts spitting in my face. I go up to wipe it but he pins my wrists behind my back and gives me another shove. I'm back on the floor like I was the day before, my head starting to bleed. He kneels down beside me and grabs a chunk of my hair.

"Stop", I say to him, my voice loud. His laugh makes me seem naive though and this time he doesn't have a split second of reminding me of him in the past. This time he knows what he is going to do. This time he executes them with no remorse. Tears slip out of my eyes as he fiercely pulls me up just to hit my head hard on the ground. I shout in pain and he repeats his motion over and over again.

Back and forth.

"Your mother birthed two weak girls", he snarls at me and I feel my head get heavy. He yanks my head again and again and this time it hurts more, it hurts like it is all new again.

Before he is able to jam my head onto the ground again, I get up. How? I look around the room and it is unfamilar. I place my hand at the back of my head and it comes back dry. My heart is beating fast in my chest and I get out of the bed trying to make sense of it all. I walk out of the room and into a dark hallway. Hands fisted at my sides, I hold my breath and walk further.

I hear loud breathing and my heart picks up fast. Where am I? I feel a doorknob and push open the door. I'm expected to see my father again sitting on the couch but I open the door to find a bed. In the bed, there is a figure sleeping. My breathing slows as I try to follow the rhythm of the other person breathing in the room. I walk into the room and toward the body.

"Oliver?", I ask in the dark. I get no reply and my hands are getting clammy. I find that I am close to the bed and my leg makes contact with the bed and I fall onto the mattress. My body awkwadly knocks into the side of his body. My hands fall on his shoulder and I shake him,"Oliver he is back."

Oliver doesn't hear me so I repeat my sentence shaking him harder. It feels too real, did I close the door behind me? On my third attempt of repeating myself, Oliver stirs under my hand. He opens his eyes and I feel my heart calm down. "He came back for me", I whisper to him and he sits up in bed quickly.

He places a hand in mine and looks around at his quiet house. He checks his phone for something and then turns to me,"Aurora?"

"Oliver", I whisper to him in the dark, my voice breaking.

"There's no one here, principessa", he says quietly and runs his hand up and down my arm. I frantically look around and chew my lip. "He came back to me and you weren't there. You were supposed to be."

"Shhh", he hums soflty and pulls me gently into bed with him. I crawl under the covers, my breaths coming uneven and I realize I've been sobbing. "It was a dream, Aurora. You're safe here." He repeats the sentences until eventually I calm down.

I place my hand on his chest,"I'm safe here?"

He pulls me close to him, connects our forehead and says,"You're safe here."

"I'm scared to fall asleep again", I say to him and he pulls me closer to him. He buries my head in his chest and then he puts the blanket over us fully.

It's dark here but I'm flushed against him and he is all I can feel. "It's just you and me, principessa", he whispers in my hair and I nod along. He runs a hand behind my back and I close my eye. He would keep me safe.

□•□□•□•

I feel the blanket get pulled off before I hear anything. "Nolan, you can't sleep in on—" The voice I recognize as his mother's voice scolding Oliver but she abruptly stops at the sight of me. Oliver still has his hands around me and I hear the soft breaths in my hair. I turn my head around at his mother looking down at us with a frown on her face.

"Rory?", she says and I manage a smile. I try to wiggle out of Oliver's arms but his hold had been tight.

"I'm sorry", I whisper to her. She doesn't say anything to me and instead calls her son again. I place a hand on his arm and try to pull him off.

"Nolan, up", his mother shouts not unkindly and Oliver stirs in his sleep. He opens his eyes, sees me, and smiles. He is about to close his eyes when I mouth his mother and he glances past me.

"Mom", he says sitting up in bed and his mother purses her lips up. "What?"

"Oh just that I'm finding my eighteen year old son in bed with a girl", she says and I feel regret wash over me. I hug my body with my hand, suddenly feeling unwelcome.

"Mom, please, we haven't even kissed within the last twenty-four hours and Aurora came in around three to my room after a nightmare. She was unsettled and I had to calm her down", Oliver says slowly and I feel warmth pass through me.

"Oh no, Rory, are you okay?", his mother says to me and I nod.

"I am. I swear I didn't come into his room for anything other than his comfort", I say quickly and his mom shakes her head.

"It's okay. Um", she looks at Oliver and I and then continues,"Just don't try anything okay?"

"Sure", Oliver says chucklikg and his mom puts a hand on her hip. "I mean it, Nolan." Oliver puts his hands up in surrender and I hop out of his bed.

"I'm sorry", I say again to her and she nods at me.

"Come down for breakfast", she says to the both of us and leaves his room. I turn around to Oliver with a frown on my face and say,"Did I ruin everything?"

"My mom is just worried. But trust me she is worried about you more than me being in bed with a girl", I recognize now that his voice is deeper now, more hoarse. His hair is also so much messier and fluffier in the morning. I feel butterflies swarm in my stomach.

"Really?", I manage to come back to the original topic. He gets out of bed and walks toward me,"Are you okay?"

"Yeah", I say feeling more calm at the wah he is looking at me. "I'm still afraid of him though."

Oliver's eyes flash with something I don't recognize and he asks,"Who is he?"

I hold my head in shame when I say,"My father."

Chapter Sixteen

Aurora

I watch as his face morphs into something so unrecognizable on him. He looks mad, his eyebrows furrowed and his jaws set. "I'm sorry, your father?" I nod and he curses under his breath.

"I knew it. That's fucking disturbing", he whispers. I looked up at him and put a hand on his chest. "I'm fine here though."

"How could a father—"

"I'm fine here", I cut him off not wanting him to make me recall the moments again. I hold his face in my hands and he presses his forehead with mine and closes his eyes. We stay like that for a very long moment before Oliver opens his eyes and I watch as he looks down. Confused to what he is looking at, I follow him and find that one of my buttons popped open exposing my breasts. My skin warms and I pull away from him, quickly trying to close it.

"If you wanted my mom to believe that we weren't doing anything, maybe you should've closed the button", he says to me his voice full of amusement.

"Oh my God", I shriek. "We weren't doing anything, though."

"I know that", he says and then smirks,"But does my mom know that?" I race out of his room silently shrieking and toward the guest room at the end of the hall. I can still hear his laugh even after I close the door.

□•□•□•□

"Morning", I say to his parents when I come down for breakfast. I put on the sweatshirt he gave me yesterday but kept the pajama pants on. His mom glances at me with a smile and his dad shares the same small smile. I look at Oliver to find him smirking. I walk past him and slap his head. He laughs and I take a seat beside him.

"I can help around the house today", I say ignoring Oliver's laughter and his attempts on holding my hand. His mom looks at me and shakes her head,"No, what?"

"Come on, I love cleaning. If you need any help, I'm free", I say to her. I turn to his father and say,"I haven't found the cream you were talking about for my ribs. Do you know where they are?"

His dad looks at me and then turns to his wife. I take the moment to take Oliver's prying hand off mine but he only holds on tighter. He laughs and I slap his hand away. He retracts it and instead grabs the pot of coffee from the table. "I left it in the drawer in your room", his mom says and I take notice of the way she used the term 'my room'. How had they been so accepting to me? It makes my heart warm.

"Oh okay", I say to her and his father gets up the table and towards Oliver's mom. I watch as he snakes a hand around her waist, whipsers something to her before planting a kiss on her lips. I blush and turn away instead to Oliver who is busy placing a toast in his mouth.

"Where is he going?", I ask and Oliver drops the toast.

"He is going out to play golf. Every weekend this follows: he eats breakfast, tells her he is going golfing, and then leaves with a fat kiss on her lips." He makes a gagging noise but I ignore him. Had my parents ever been this affectionate toward each other? I can't remember a time where they hugged unless it was for a holiday.

"I don't think my parents were ever in love", I say to him quietly.

"Had to be, they had two kids", Oliver says nonchalantly and I shrug.

"I've never seen them hug, maybe at a time they were but then they weren't. That terrifies me", I admit. Oliver places a toast on my plate and says, "What does?"

"Falling out of love", I whisper and he looks at me abruptly. His eyes flash with something before he looks away. "If I fell out of love with somebody I'd feel...well I don't know."

"I wouldn't fall out of love with you", Oliver says and it makes the both of us silent. Is he initiating that he is falling in love with me? That scares me. I glance over at him to find that his ears are flushed and his cheek has a slight tint to it. The conversation ends and his mother comes back to the room which I hadn't even noticed she left in the first place.

"What is going on here?", Victoria says noticing our silence.

"Nothing", Oliver says quickly and I look down at my food. I pick up the toast and place it in my mouth. It surprisingly goes down my stomach faster than I would've thought and it makes me feel a little pride at my accomplishment.

"Rory, I do have to vacuum. Do you want to do it?", Victoria says and I nod at the aspect of being helpful.

"Thank you", she says and then walks back out of the room. Oliver and I eat in silence, his words playing over and over in my head, no doubt his also.

Does Oliver have deeper feelings for me?

□•□•□□•

Oliver and I are yet again watching more Disney movies. Well he is, I'm doing his homework. I sigh at the fact that I'm going to have so much homework to redo tomorrow. He takes about the same classes as me but he isn't in the same class. I breeze through his homework casually looking at the tv at times.

After our third movie, he picks up the remote and throws it on the other couch after having turned off the tv.

"It's so boring", he complains as I put his homework in the folder. I cross my arms over my chest and say,"Well."

"Come on, let's do something", he says grabbing my hand.

"I don't want to go out today", I say frowning and he nods.

"No, I know that. Is there anything else we can do?", he says and I try to think of better options.

"I don't think so", I say to him. He sighs, runs a hand over his hair, and then looks at me. He has a triumphant smile on his face and within a second, he is charging for me. My complaints die in my throat as his hands shimmy up and down my torso feather light making me laugh.

I shriek when his hands make their way under my hoodie to get better access. He only chuckles and moves his hand around my belly button area. The feeling of his hands on my bare skin makes me quiet down for a second. He looks down at me, he is also silent all of a sudden, his eyes intensely meeting mine. He glances down at my lip and mine follow, he starts to lean in but I turn around and face the couch.

I feel him move off of me and I regret the absence of his presence. Did I hurt his feelings? I sit up and find him moving toward his homework to put it away even though I already did that. I put my hands behind my leg and say,"I'm sorry, Oliver."

"For what, principessa?", he says quietly looking at me and I bite my bottom lip.

"I'm leading you on. And the thing is I actually do want to kiss you", I whisper,"Again."

"So what's stopping you?", he says, his eyes fixated on me, so luring, but he makes no move of walking toward me.

"I don't know", I say and walk towards him. I place my hand on his chest and feel his heart beat picking up so fast under my hand. "This."

"What?", he whispers, challenging me to share my honest words with him.

"I'm going to hurt you", I say and he shakes his head. His eyes flit down to my lips again and he brings it back up to my eyes.

"I'll take my chances", he says keeping eye contact with me, giving me the option whether to kiss him or not. He had tried once and this time he wants me to be the one to make a move. I freeze for a second, thinking out my options. But then I think about the reason I'm not kissing him, and I try to find a good reason. He is nice, he is caring, he is handsome and he is so gentle with me. So what's stopping me? I can't figure it out.

So, I stand on my tiptoes and put my hand on his neck, pulling him toward me. Our lips meet in a soft embrace and he exhales in my mouth. He moves his lips faster against me and I feel an eager adrenaline pass around me. I pull our bodies closer together, his hands tightening around my waist. I'm about to kiss him back harder when a voice pulls us apart.

I put my hand behind my back, instantly dropping my hands from him. I find his mom standing there with a vacuum. "Um", she says and then clears her throat,"Nolan?"

"Mom", he says softly and I bite my bottom lip to not laugh at his obliviousness.

"We need to keep the kissing to a minimum", his mom says and I nod. I look back at Oliver and he shakes his head. His mother raises an eyebrow and Oliver smiles,"I mean sure."

"Right", she says giving him a look and then turning to me.

"Come on, Rory. Let's let my son catch his breath", she sends me a prideful smile and I can't help but smile at that.

I look back at Oliver who waves at me, a big grin plastered on his face. I place my hand on my lip and wave with my other hand. He chuckles and I smile.

Oliver has made his way into my heart and I couldn't do anything to stop him.

Chapter Seventeen

O^{liver}

Waking up in the morning and finding Aurora sitting in the kitchen is something I've come to enjoy far more than I'd like to admit. She looks cute with her hair tied back in a bun and in the matching pajama set I bought for her. As I watch her closely, a smile takes over my face. I know what this translates to: mine. She looks like mine sitting at the table talking to my mom while absentmindedly caressing a pancake on her plate.

I walk over to her and place a gentle hand on her eye from behind. I feel her flinch under my touch and retract my hand quick. I lean down and press a kiss on the side of her head and whisper, "I'm sorry, principessa." It genuinely hurt when I saw her flinch at my unannounced touch. She is still nursing a fear and I've come to play with it unintentionally.

I walk around to her and instead of frowning, she smiles softly at me. She moves a hand up and waves at me, and I try not to swoon at the sight. Hot. I glance at my mom and feel my cheek warm at the thought. My mom scolds me when I try to grab a plate and says, "You've got school, if you wanted food you should have woken up earlier."

I frown and my mom only shakes her head and turns away.

"Can I go to school, too?", I hear her voice suddenly more closer to me and turn around to find her approaching me. She reaches out a hand to touch my arm and I let her wrap her delicate hand around it.

"Are you sure?", my mom asks and she nods leaning close to me, her head resting on my arm. "Well, if you're sure", my mom shrugs,"Your head still bother you?"

Aurora shrugs,"I've gone to school in much more pain." I wince at her words and my mind flashes to all of the mornings I picked her up from school, her shoulders were slumped and she had a frown on her face. I should've known. I should've seen all the sign. I don't regret giving Aurora her privacy, but I should've seen it.

"After school, I was thinking of stopping by my house and grabbing a few things. He won't be there until thirty minutes later", she says quietly.

"I can't risk that", my mom says and I nod with her.

"I'll skip practice for the beginning and drive you there", I say to her and she nods appreciatingly at me. My mom places a hand on her hip and still frowns. "I'm coming with you. He hurt you so bad, Rory. I'm letting letting anything happen to you."

"I agree", I add agreeing with my mom and Aurora's eyes fill with tears. I take a step back but she only digs her face into the crook of my arm. "Are you having cold feet?" I ask her and she shakes her head.

"You guys are too nice", she says softly and I melt at her words. She is coming close to tears at the expense of us being kind, decent.

"It's hardly bare minimum", I say to her and she shakes her head again. She looks up at me and stands on her tip toes and says,"Thank you." I nod at her and she leans up and places a kiss close to my lip. I like the feeling of her lips on my face, it makes my stomach flutter with something I've never felt before.

She turns to my mom,"Thank you also. I uh I've never known someone who could welcome a complete stranger to their home." I wipe the tear off of her face and take notice that her eyes are a much lighter shade of green today.

"My son cares for you; I care for you then", and with that my mom signals for me to head upstairs to change. I grab Aurora's hand and lead her up to my room. Once I get in, I grab a change of clothes and say,"Go get ready. Come back to my room and I'll see what I can do about your outfit."

"Okay", she says and walks out of the room. I head to my bathroom and do my routine. I change into clothes and walk out to find Aurora standing next to my bed running hand through her hair. I close the distance between us and lean down to kiss her, suddenly wanting to feel her against me. She tastes of fresh mint and I want to kiss her deeply, but she places a hand on my chest. I pull away and look down at her.

I walk away with a hand running down the length of her hair toward my closet. I sift through my clothes to come up shorts on bottoms but find a soft green shirt. I hand it to her but she looks up at me and places her hand on my chest again. Can she feel my rapid heartbeats?

"I like your shirt better", she whispers and is that a tone I haven't heard in her voice before? Is she flirting with me? The soft tone of her voice and the way her smile deepens at the end tells me I'm right.

"Yeah?", I whisper to her taunting her. She nods, biting her bottom lip. "Well what are you going to do about it?", I say, bold. Her hands find the hem of my shirt and she starts lifting it up over my torso. I watch her in amusement as she pulls it over my arms and over my head. She fists up the shirt and leans in and places a gentle kiss on my chest, making my muscles tense up.

"Aurora", I whisper her name sounding breathless.

"There you go", she says before throwing me the shirt I offered her. I catch it and throw it over my head and my arms. When I look at her I find that the shirt I'm wearing is the same shade as her eyes. I smirk at her and she smiles. I know that she wanted me to wear it to match her eyes and I'm not complaining, I love it.

A knock on the door pulls my attention off of the girl in front of me. I find my mom standing at the doorway with a pair of leggings in her hand. "The dryer shrunk these so I'm guessing it'll fit." Aurora walks over to her and takes the pants out of her hand.

She glances back at me and says, "I'll see you in the car?" I nod and she walks out of the room to change.

□•□•□•□

Aurora manages to survive the school day without a backpack. She was so worried that the teachers would yell at her, but she found out that a notebook and a pencil is all she needs. How does she think a lot of the kids pass school nowadays? After school, I find my coach and inform him of my expected tardiness. He lets me off on a warning and I grab Aurora's hand and head to my car.

Aurora looks out the window for most of the ride and I look at her when I pull into her driveway. There isn't another car parked there but that doesn't stop her from fidgeting with the sleeve of her shirtsleeve. We wait for my mom and when I see her car pull up, Aurora flinches.

"My mom", I whisper to her and she nods even though her eyes are still wild. I open our doors and the both of us walk out. My mom gets out of the car too and with my hand in hers, I lead her to the porch. Her hands are shaky as she uses the lock to open the door. I wish I could calm her but this isn't something that I could fix. This was caused by years of abuse and that's not something that disappears within a second.

She let's out a shaky breath and opens the door wide. She walks into the house and I feel my heart clench for her. She takes a few steps in, finds the spot she was laying on and turns back to me so abruptly I'm surprised.

"Get me out of here", she whispers and buries her head in my chest, all of her body weight on me. I put a hand on her waist and pull her out of the house. She looks up at me and says,"I thought I was strong enough for it." Tears are rapidly falling out of her eyes and I can't wipe fast enough for them to not fall.

"Mom, go in there. Get all her clothes, she is never stepping in here again", I say to her and Aurora sobs louder in my chest. I run a hand through her hair and whisper sweet nothings in her hair.

"Principessa. We'll never let you go in there", I say to her and she claws at my shirt, wanting to believe me. "I promise", I say and feel her nod against my chest. My mom gets back a few moments later with three bags full of stuff. She also has a backpack perched on her shoulders.

"I'm sorry", my mom whispers and walks to her car. She throws the bags in the trunk and turns to us.

"Come on, Rory, let's get you away from here. Nolan, you're going to be okay at practice today?", she says and I nod not realizing a tear has slipped out of my eye. My heart hurts for the girl in my arms. With a last sniffle, she walks out of my arm and toward my mom. My mom immediately places a hand on her shoulder and leads her into the passenger side door. I watch as Aurora glances at her house one last time before sobbing once more.

I wipe my face and get into my own car before I break down in front of her. The urge to make her dad hurt is so strong as I drive down to the school with my hands fisted tightly on the steering wheel.

Chapter Eighteen

Aurora

"Do you think you can honestly hide from you?", his voice is booming even as I put a hand on my ear to shut him out. "I will find you."

"No you won't", my voice is barely above a whisper.

He laughs, an ugly sound,"I will. That boyfriend of yours won't be able to protect you. He has other responsibilities. He can't be by your side forever. And honestly that's pathetic."

"Oliver is my best friend", I say and that prompts him to laugh harder.

"He will leave you once he realizes how needy you are. Why would he keep you around? Use you, protect you, and then dump you. Only time will tell."

"No he won't", I say my hands balled up in a fist.

"Only time will tell. In the meantime, I'm still coming for you", he says and starts making a move toward me. I try to run away but when I turn around Oliver is there. I start toward him but he moves me toward my monster of a father. Tears spring in my eye at his betryal and my father charges at me.

I wake up with a jolt, sweat beading past my forehead. I feel it drip down my face and onto my neck. That felt too real. I claw at my blanket and pull it off me. I walk toward my door and open the two locks Oliver helped me install the other day. Once I get it open, I make my way to his room. I find him in bed and I want to reach out to him. Hold onto him. But if I touch him, I won't be able to leave his arms and I respect his mom enough to know I shouldn't sleep in his bed with him.

Instead, I lean down and a place a kiss on his forehead. His muscles tense at my touch and I whisper,"Grazie piccolo."

Thank you, baby.

I leave his room with the door closed behind me and head to my room where I know that I will stare at the ceiling until the sun rises. It's never easy for me to fall back asleep after my daily nightmares.

□□•□•□••

It is lunchtime and the team has all gathered together at our table making me sit on Oliver's lap. I hang off his one leg while he keeps a hand on my waist, steadying me.

"What do you think, principessa?", he says to me when the team starts arguing at a certain point. I look up at him and say,"Sorry, what?"

He tickles my waist and says,"Not paying attention?"

"I'm sorry", I say to him and he puts a hand on my lip neutralizing my pout.

"Do you think Austin should do a cartwheel on the court when we win?", he says and the whole team starts laughing. I look up at Austin who is shaking his head and with my eye on his, I nod.

"Yes", I say and the crowd of people around us cheers so loud I don't have anything to pull me down to reality but Oliver's arm under my shirt. I found that that is his favorite thing to do when we are eating, watching tv, or even simply standing. He draws circles on my skin and I take a deep breath in.

"Did you eat?", he whispers in my hair and I nod. I ate a little, just fries but enough that he doesn't need to be worried about me. "Good girl", he draws out the words and my stomach erupts in butterflies.

"You guys are disgusting", Austin says feigning a gag and Oliver flashes his middle finger at him.

"Find yourself a girl and then come back to me?", he says his mouth is still in my hair. I hear Austin gag harder and I flash my middle finger at him too.

"No way!", Austin laughs and a guy on the team slaps him on the back. I smile triumphant at him and laughs.

"Oliver man, she turned just like you", he says and Oliver laughs into my hair.

□•□□••□

I'm watching my boyfriend- we haven't made it official yet but judging by our constant kissing it should be an unspoken thing- play basketball while I do homework. I'm more focused on the way he moves on court though, steady and strategically. He catches me looking at him and throws me a wink. I wish I could kiss him while he is throwing a hoop. The fantasy makes butterflies erupt in my stomach.

My phone dings with a notification from a restaurant just a block from Oliver's house. I need to get a job to pay back his parents for allowing me to stay in their house. I brought it up to Oliver a few days ago briefly and he informed me that his parents make enough to have saved up for his colelege since he was 13 and that they would be able to pay regardless but

I shook my head. I hadn't been able to object further when he bent down and connected our lips together. I didn't complain about it though because Oliver knew how to kiss.

He knew how to make me yearn for more, he knew how to warm my body up with just a chaste kiss on my lip. I'm falling for him, I realized in the middle of our makeout yesterday night. The thought would have scared me but I welcomed it. Well, I had to, seeing as Oliver had his tongue down my throat. I wonder if he would be this affectionate with me all the time.

I type back a reply to the job saying to come in tomorrow for an interview and go back to watching Oliver play. I'm so immersed in my task that I don't hear someone take s seat beside me. The person breathes and that's when I feel my heart beat quicken. I look to my right and watch my eyes reflect back at me.

I hadn't admitted it to Oliver but the day we went back to grab my stuff, I saw him in a car when we were pulling away. He had made eye contact with me and I had flinched inside of the car. His eyes told me that he would be back, and now here he was.

"Aurora", he says and I try to leave. His hand finds both of mine and pins them down on his lap, making me gag at the contact of his genitals. He looks down at me and says,"Where the fuck did you go?"

I don't say anything but look ahead at Oliver who is too into the game to see me. I'm about to open my mouth to shout his name when his other hand clams my mouth. I feel blood rush to my head and my heart beating quick.

"You think you can leave me?", he says and I shake my head violently. My fear had come true, I've been dreading this moment. His hand on my mouth presses harder and he yanks me harder to pull me off the seat. I try my best to resist but can't when be pulls me off the stadium. I don't know what to do. I should be stronger than this but I'm not.

His grip on my wrists tighten and he pulls me toward under the bleachers. This is where Oliver and I kissed just yesterday when he had a moment of free time. The thought makes me want to scream for him, but the hand tightens around my mouth.

"You made a huge mistake", he says and gives me not a second before he jams his forehead against mine making me wince in pain. The head that worked so hard to heal this past week throbs again. He yanks my hair and with my free hands I press them against his chest. That causes him to release his hold on my mouth and I shout like I've never shouted before.

So loud his eyes flash with fear before his fist connects with my jaw and I feel blood in my mouth. I scream even louder now and he keeps punching me. Over and over again.

God, can't he be original?

He laughs once he realizes I have given up. My body hurts to stand and I've been resting my head against the bleachers. He is about to punch me again and I close my eye tight but open them when I realize the punch never came. I look forward to seeing Oliver standing there with my dads hand and in a second, he twists his wrist and I hear my dad groan in agony.

I blink once, not believing this but this is true. Oliver punches my fathers face so hard that my father staggers backward. My boyfriend punches him again and this time he falls to the ground. He makes a move to sit up but Oliver connects his shoe to his chest. "Try and fucking move, bitch."

I watch as my dad's eyes roll to the back of his head before his eyes shut. Oliver spits at the ground beside him and says,"Try and fucking touch her again. I'll knock you out faster next time." He kicks him on the chest, making my father groan once more opening his eyes to look up at Oliver. Oliver stares right back,"Don't you ever touch her again. Remember that."

With that, he steps off of him and rushes toward me. His hands find myface and he puts a hand on either side of my jaw and I wince in pain. "That motherfuker", he whispers and I groan in pain. "Principessa", he looks hurt at the noise and places his hand on my waist helping me move. I lean my head against the crook of his neck, not being able to stand up right. A hand grabs at my leg and I shout again. Oliver looks down at my leg and his shoe connects with my fathers face making him drop his hand.

"Get me out of here", I whisper to him and he does. He pulls me out from under the bleacher and toward his team who is all now looking at us in confusion.

"Call my dad", Oliver shas and the team looks at me frozen. "Call my dad", Oliver shouts louder. He turns to me and looks me in the eye,"You're going to be okay."

"I don't know", I'm sobbing. I'm not sure when I started but tears are rolling down my cheek rapidly.

"You're going to be okay", he says slowly nodding along to his words. I let out a shaky breath and he uses a finger to run a hand down my cheek,"My strong principessa."

"Oliver", I whisper his name looking stright at his hazel eyes and wondering how I got here. I feel his hands tighten around me before I pass out again.

There was hope in his eyes, and I'm holding on to that.

Chapter Nineteen

Aurora

I wake up looking at hazel eyes so familiar they warm my heart. Within a second, it comes back to me. "He came back", I whisper my eyes frantic and my hands going around his neck. I cling to him and he pulls me into his chest. I move onto his lap and hold on to him tight.

"He told me he would be back", I say and pull away. When I look up at him, I see his expression so sad I feel like crying. "He told you that?"

I nod,"In my dream." I watch as his face morphs into confusion, eyebrows downcast, brows furrowed.

"You've been having nightmares?", he asks and I nod. "Every night."

"Every night?", he questions and looks past me. I look back to find his parents sitting down on the other couch, worried looks on their faces. His dad looks at me and says,"Are they bad?"

I play with the hair on the nape of Oliver's neck and say,"I wake up in sweat and my heart doesn't calm down until after I get out of bed and walk into

Oliver's room." I don't even feel ashamed at the fact that I mentioned how I walk toward his room. How I look for Oliver for a sense of peace.

"You need to be medicated", his father says ignoring my previous comment. I nod at him and his mom starts crying.

"Victoria, no", I say but I watch as tears slip down her eyes. Her husband puts a supporting hand around her shoulder and I watch her sob against him. "Tell me", she says,"Tell me the whole story."

"Mom", Oliver says, trying to protect me so I didn't have to tell the story. I look at him. He gives me a small smile and I lean up and kiss his lips.

I turned back to Victoria,"The night he attacked me I had just gotten back from a party I went with Oliver. It was around one a.m and when he saw me walk into the house, he grabbed me. His hands made their way down to the zipper of my hoodie and he pulled it down to reveal my corset top. It was revealing."

"No", his mom says and I feel Oliver stiffen under me. He must feel guilty knowing he wanted me to wear that. But I don't regret it. It made me feel confident and I even got to talk to a few girls who complimented me. It was a memory I cherished.

"He said that my mother used to wear clothes like these in Italy and that she used to", I stop take a deep breath and say,"Seduce younger guys and let them do whatever they wanted to her. He said she used to sleep with a different one every night."

"To you?", his father asks and I nod.

"And then he said that I was the same. He said that", I stop and look at Oliver. His eyes are already on me and I look away. "He said that I let Oliver do whatever he wanted with me." His parents look at me with horror at the assumption that their son would do a thing. I shook my head,"I objected. Wait, my memory is bad. This was before, but uh and then he moved on and said that my family left me because I wasn't worth it. He said that Frankie, my sister, left me and wasn't going to come back. and I also objected to that and he said it was true. And then he started talking about my mom whoring around again and I said he was lying."

"He pushed me so hard I fell on the ground and then he kicked my ribs a few times, laughing. I told him to stop once I was throwing up blood, and he came down and asked me what I said. I said stop again and he looked at me, and for a split second I saw my father again. I saw it in his eyes how much he used to care about me."

"Principessa", I hear Oliver say to me and I look up at him. I smile,"I really did. I saw all our memories together and I prayed that it would bring him back. Back to the days where he would wait for me after school to hug me. But", I stop and hiccup. "That all was that: hope. He blinked and then slammed my head against the ground. I threw up again and that gave him satisfaction and he kept going. Over and over again. Fisting my hair in his hand and slamming it against the floor until eventually I passed out."

I stop and take a deep breath in,"God knows what he did next."

"What do you mean?", three voices ask me at the same time and I close my eyes. I didn't want to think about it but it could've happened. With him, anything could have happened.

I look down on the floor when I say,"He uh sexualized me. He would touch me and stuff. I would stay in my room when he would drink so he wouldn't touch me. But I wasnt able to do that at all times."

"That motherfucker", Oliver whispers in my ear and I nod. I take a deep breath in and say,"Once he got mad at me for being with Oliver that he, well, he kissed my neck. He kissed my neck continuously until I got a hickey."

My nickname and my names were said in horror and I shook off the memory, it was one that haunted for every night.

"He branded me so I wouldn't stay around Oliver. It was well", I stop talking and instead place my hands back on Oliver's neck. I bury my head in his chest and feel his heart beat rapidly. He runs a hand on my back and I feel myself calm down.

"I'm going to kill him", he whispers to me and I sob. A loud, ugly sound. We stay like that until I eventually pick up my head and look at his parents. They both have horror on their faces and I attempt a smile to them.

"Rory, you know none of that was your fault?", Victoria says. "Your clothing never should've made him put a hand on you. I'm sorry."

"No, I know. I know that it wasn't entirely my fault. I was just the last person in my family left for him to terrorize", I say.

"He did it to Frankie?", Oliver asks and I nod. "He was sexual with her way before he was with me. When she was here all I saw were the little comments but when she left for college, he started treating me worse. Touching me. I then realized she went through it too."

"Oh my God", his mother cries and I can't help by cry with her.

"She's in Italy now. She won't come back. she's safe."

"She left you", Oliver says and I turn to him. "I'm sorry, but she left you. How could she? She knew you were going to be next."

"She had to protect herself", I say.

"She would've taken you with her", Oliver says anger dripping off of him at the fact that there was nobody there to protect me.

"She wasn't strong enough", I say and Oliver nods. He pulls me into his chest again, only this time pulls me up until our heads meet.

"I'm sorry, la mia principessa", he whispers to me and despite his parents watching us, he connects his lips with mine. I melt into his kiss but he lets go way too early. He connects our foreheads together and says,"I promise to never leave you. Ti amo." The phrase in my native language makes my heart melt.

He loves me. He loves me.

"Ti amo?", I ask him and he presses a kiss on my forehead. "Ti amo, Aurora."

" I uh", I say and he shakes his head.

"Not for me. You don't have to say anything. I'm saying this for you. I'll love you for the both of us. Ti amo", he repeats and I feel a tear slip down my cheek.

A cough distracts us from our silent confession and I look back to see his parents standing. His mom nods at me and says,"Rory, I'm calling the police right now."

"Wait what?", I say and then say,"I can't give my statement right now." It was hard enough sharing this with the three of them, but in a room with adults? Without being in Oliver's lap? I couldn't do it.

"No this is for a restraining order against him", she says and I nod knowing that this is the one thing I need. One thing that might keep me away from him, safe.

His parents leave and I look up at Oliver. "Can I fall asleep on your lap?", I ask and he nods. "Any day", he says and I lean up and kiss him on the lip before leaving one on his neck.

"Thank you", I say to him and he nods. I place my hand in his and hold it to my heart. Oliver didn't know it, but he was the reason I was still holding on and I had to thank him for that.

Chapter Twenty

O liver

Aurora fell asleep on my lap a few hours ago and I haven't moved much just when I layed down, pulling her with me. She now whimpers against my chest, fighting off whatever monsters she is facing in her mind. Of course, now I know who the monster is and I want to punch him. Again. The way he chooses a teenaged girl as his victim is distrubing—disgusting.

I should've punched him more but I had wanted to get Aurora away from him as soon as possible. I wanted her to be safe and away from him. Watching her look at my so tenderly and then pass out is something that haunts me. She looked at me like I was her light and then darkness came over her and she left. It took my dad a while to get here and once he did, we made a beeline home.

And that's how he escaped. The son of a bitch wasn't worth our energyto fight. We were only merely interested in getting Aurora safely home to take care of her. I'm about to close my eye when I hear footsteps enter the room. I look up to see my mom walking in with Austin behind her.

She looks at me apologetically knowing that I asked her to have no guests. I turn to Austin and he makes his way and takes a seat on the other couch, taking a seat.

"What are you doing here?", I ask him softly rubbing a hand on Aurora's back when she starts clawing at my chest with her hand. Austin runs a hand down his face and blows out a raspberry.

"I came to check on you", he says and I feel myself scoffing.

"And why is that?", I ask and Austin shrugs.

"You were so exhausted after everything that went down and I wanted to see if you were doing okay", he says and glances down at the girl laying on my chest. She had calmed down now, her hands making their way toward my neck. I smile when her hand plays with my hair.

"I'm fine. I was just worried about Aurora", I say and Austin nods.

He plays with his hand and says, "Was that really her dad?" I nod and Austin frowns. I know seeing the after math of the incident earlier today had to have shaken him up too considering he had a father who was abuse. Not to him though, to his mother, but Austin had gotten involved when he couldn't let his mother get hurt anymore. He took the beatings for her until one day he went to school a few years ago and the counselars asked him about it.

He refused to answer but they persisted and two days later, his father was being dragged out of the house and into a police car. His mother had been so shaken up that she couldn't care for herself or Austin that they came over to my house to stay for a week. My mom helped his mother where as I tried to get my hest freind to smile. It took him a few days but I got him to smile.

Austin has been grateful for me ever since, never once taking me for grant- ed. I loved that about him, he would still be humble even though now he has everything and beyond. He has a step father who still pays eveything for him despite Austin asking him to not bother. His step father takes them on a vacation at least once a year and makes sure to carve time for his mom with work and everything.

But Austin never forgets about what his father did to him and so he always turns back to me to give back. Him being here against my judgement is a way for him to give back.

"Oli", he starts and looks at Aurora, who is now making her way up my chest and into the crook of my neck, "Know that I'm here for you. For Rory. I can find the lawyers that did my father's case."

"I'll ask Aurora about it and get back to you. And thank you, really", I say to him offering him a smile. The girl in my arms starts to stir and I watch as she looks up at me. Her lips curve up and just before she is about to lean up and kiss me, I say,"Austin's here."

I watch in amusement as Aurora picks herself off of me and sitting up. She pulls down her clothes and looks at Austin who is smiling softly at her. "How are you feeling?", my best friend asks my girlfriend and she shrugs.

"I'm feeling better. Tired", her words are soft reminding me of when I first saw her. When we were first talking she would share no more than two words per sentence.

"That's good. You're strong", he says and then stands up from the spot on the couch. "Oli, man. I should get going but I'll see you at school?"

I nod and he waves at Aurora. "Bye, Rory."

She only waves back at him and then turns to me with a soft frown. "He came back for me", she says and I frown as well but nodding nonetheless.

"I saw", I say, pulling her toward me and placing a hand on her face,"You stirred a lot and whimpered."

She frowns deeper,"I wish I could dream about you."

"Oh yeah?", I say sounding like the teenaged guy I am. But Aurora only nods,"I want to dream of you hugging me, holding me, kissing me. The things you do to make me feel better."

"Aw, principessa", I say, the Italian nickname I learned from her rolling off my tongue. "In the meantime, let me fulfill those dreams." I place both of my arms around her waist and pull her close to me. Once she is close enough, I lean down and meet my lips with hers. With her injuries, our kiss is more stiff but enjoyable nonetheless. I always enjoy every moment I have with her.

I pull away once her breathing starts to waver and instead pull her in for a hug. Her hands go to my neck and she hides her head behind it. I love her like this, so clingy. "Is this the dream you were hoping for?", I whisper.

"Everything and more", she whipsers back making my stomach dip in the warmth of her words. We stay like that for a while until my parents come down to tell us to get some food for us. It's been so long since I've eaten and at the mention of it, my stomach growls. I take Aurora's hand and lead us through the small hallway and into the kitchen.

We find my parents eating at the counter so we take a seat on the table where our plate full of pasta waits for us. I grab a fork and dig in, my mouth watering at my favorite home cooked meal. I'm halfway done when I look to my right to find Aurora glaring at the food like it disgusts her.

"Principessa?", I ask and she blinks one time before turning to me. She plasters on a fake smile and picks up her fork. I know her well enough to know the food would never get to her stomach. I pick up my fork and get a good scoop and take it toward her mouth. Her full mouth juts up in a pout but I only place it on her lip, she eventually opens her mouth and takes the content on my fork. I watch as she slowly chews and places a soft hand on her shoulder to coax her into chewing.

She does and I feel a smile tug all the way up to my eyes. Pride. I've never been proud of someone more than I've been with Aurora. "Can you eat for me, Aurora?"

She nods and then tugs a piece of hair behind her ear. She's suddenly shy when she asks,"I'm sorry if it seems a little...babyish. But I'd prefer it if you would feed me. It helps me to actually eat."

"I'd be happy too", and I was. I helped her finish off her whole plate. It took a long time but eventually she did it. We place our plates in the sink and when we are about to head to watch some television, my parents stop us.

"Aurora, I can't prescribe you medicine unless you come in to the hospital", my dad says.

Aurora twirls a piece of her hair between two fingers and thinks. She takes a deep breath and says,"I can come in tomorrow after school. I have to go to a job interview afterwards though."

"No worries, I'll sign you in ealier then. Also, why the job interest?", my dad asks and my mom nods along with him. She looks at me and then at the floor and I realize she is blushing.

"I love your guys' kindness. I do", she says her eyes moving up to my parents,"But I can't let you guys pay for everything when I can get a job."

"True. A job is important for you but don't worry about paying us back. You just getting better is all we can ask in return. Save up the money for the future, I'm sure you'll need it", my mom says to her her voice kind.

"No, I want to pay you back", my girlfriend says.

My mom shakes her head,"You getting better and making my son happy is all I expect from you."

Mom. I feel a little blush creep up at the fact that my mom is embarassing me.

"Okay", she says to my parents and then turns to me. "I'm paying them back", she whispers to only my ears and I bite back a smile. She is so stubborn for her own good.

"Nolan", my dad says dragging my attention away from the girl in front of me. "Aurora can sleep in your room if she wants."

"Really?", I ask suprised but not trying to show too much eagerness.

My mom shakes her head, smiling a little,"Yes, the door stays open though and tops stay on. And bottoms."

"Mom", I say feeling my cheeks really heat up now and when I glance at Aurora, she has turned fully red. She looks up at my mom, blows out her cheek and says,"Of course."

"Thank you. Keep him in check, yeah?", my mom says, making me groan and turn more red. With a last wave, they both head upstairs and we head toward the living room to digest our food for a bit. After a couple episodes of Modern family, we head upstairs as well.

Aurora changes into one of my shirts and a pair of shorts and comes back to my room. I am brushing my teeth when she hops into bed and pulls the sheets up to her. She then lays on her side and looks at me with a soft smile on her face. I love you, my heart screams at her. She is looking at me like I'm her whole world and that makes my heart clench. Once I spit the toothpaste out, I turn off the light and walk toward the bed.

I get in and Aurora turns to me. "Does your head still hurt, baby?"

"Yeah", she whispers and I hate how her head throbbing has become natural to her. I place my hand on her forehead and say a quick prayer. I pull my hand back and instead scoot closer to her.

"Get some rest, yeah?"

"I will, Oli", she says throwing her hand over me. I laugh and pull her toward me with a hand on her waist.

"You're mine, you know that?", I say and she bites her bottom lip.

"I'm yours", she agrees and my head spins at how adorable she looks right now. "And you're mine?"

"You know it", I say and lean down to press a kiss to her temple. I hear her giggling beneath me and I close my eyes, falling asleep to the sound of her happiness. I hope that tonight she gets to dream of something happy instead of the monster that tortured her for the last four years. I don't know how parents can turn awful once something happens to them and their children become inconveniences.

What happened to unconditional love? The promise to keep your child safe the moment they take their first birth? What happned to morals?

It's all wrong. So wrong. I can't imagine a world where my parents do so much as threaten me. They adore me as they should and I couldn't be more grateful for that.

I'm determined to show Aurora unconditional love, the love that is so eternal that even in the worst of our fights, our love for each other is strong enough to turn us toward the right path.

If Aurora loves me, that is.

Chapter Twenty- One

A urora

I love him; it's as simple as that. I'm not sure why I didn't say it yesterday, but I feel it as true as daylight. When I woke up in the middle of the night after yet another nightmare, I opened my eyes to find Oliver next to me. I had somehow wiggled out of his arms so I scooted closer to him and placed myself at the crook of his arm.

My heart still racing from the nightmare, I lifted my hand up to his face and traced his features. His nose is straight but not too long and his cupid bow is longer rather than a tiny space and his jawline was sharp agaisnt my finger. I loved him, I loved his face. Not more than his heart though.

"Oliver?", I say to him in the dark trying to find comfort but cannot. I place my hand on his chest and pat him. He opens his eyes, frantic eyes as he tries to make sense of what happened. He finds me looking at him and visibly relaxes, throwing an arm around my waist.

"Another one?", he whispers and I nod. He sighs, a long depressing one, and tucks a piece of hair behind my ear. "I'm here, principessa. Don't let him get to you. I'll be here."

I frown at his niceness but he only smiles at me. I place my head on his chest and take a deep breath in. I inhale and exhale a few times before looking up at him. I love you, I want to say. Instead, I let him pull me closer to him and throw a leg over his torso. I close my eye and wait for sleep to take me. I eventually fell asleep with the sound of his heart beating under me. So relaxing that mine follows.

□•□•□•□•

I decided to skip school the next day seeing as my head still throbbed when I woke up. That made Oliver's dad move my appointment earlier to 11 o'clock. Oliver had frowned at the fact that he would have to go back to school where as I would he able to go back to his room and hide under the covers.

"I'll miss you", he says when I laugh at him. I'm already in his bed with the blanket pulled up to my chest. "I'm sure you are going to be bored without me."

I shake my head, smiling instead. Oliver looks hotter today or is it because I've been staring at him this whole morning? I watched him do his hair this morning, which consists of washing and blow drying. He put in oil that made his hair shine and that prompted me to stare at it for a while. He is also dressed nicely today: White colored shirt with a blue sweatshirt over it. Since when did he dress that way? It makes me want to pull him by his collar in for a kiss.

The thought makes me let out an involuntary giggle and feeling my face warm at the thought, I cover myself with the blanket. I hear Oliver's footsteps approaching me and not long after, he pulls the blanket away from my face.

"What's so funny?", he says and I shake my head, my hair falling into my eye. Oliver places his backpack onto his other shoulder and uses his hand to move the hair off my face and behind my ear. I watch as a small smile appears at the sight of my face. He leans down, his head making its way toward my ear. "What was it, principessa?" I shake my head and his groan is loud in my ear, causing goosebumps to pass down my body.

I shake my head again and he leans away and runs a hand through his hair. "Guess I'll just—" He doesn't get a chance to finish his sentence because when I lean up and grab a hold of his collar, his eyes widen. I bite my lip from letting out a smile and pull him down crashing our lips together. He lets out a gasp in my mouth and I smile wider. Once he starts to get to the rhythm of the kiss, I can feel my heart calming down.

His phone buzzes on the table and he groans pulling away from me not before I grab his bottom lip in between my teeth making him widen his eye when I do pull away. I fall back down on the bed, my breaths coming in uneven. Grabbing his phone, he turns to me and says,"That was hot, Aurora." My name and the word hot in the same sentence is foreign to my ears but I welcome his words with a smile. "That was crazy hot", he says making me blush harder.

He leans down and presses a gentle kiss on my forehead. "Have a good day, okay?", he says and I nod. He walks away as I wave at him. Before he walks out of the doorway though, he turns around and says,"Was that what you were giggling about?"

"I don't kiss and tell", I say biting down on my bottom lip. His face lights up like a Christmas tree at my words as he smiles wide. I laugh and with a final wave, he leaves. That was the most wholesome moment we've had in our relationship. I loved it, God, I love him. I fall back asleep with a smile on my face, the blanket smelling like him.

A couple hours later, I am awake again. I had walked to my room in Oliver's house and picked out some jeans for the day. I wore a tank top and then started walking over to Oliver's room. I found his dad walking up the stairs though and hugged myself with my arms, exposing this much skin around a male makes feel anxious. His dad keeps his eyes on mine though and says,"Almost done?"

"Yeah", I say edging toward Oliver's room. "Give me a minute", I add. His dad nods and then looks away from me. I follow his eyes to find that he had looked down on the floor and the fact that he hadn't once glanced at my torso made me smile. Is this what a solid nice man looked like? Respectful?

I nodded at him and headed over to Oliver's room. I walked into his closet and pulled out a light blue hoddie. I slipped into it and bunched up the hem of it to make it look smaller on me. I snapped a photo of myself and texted it to Oliver on my phone that Victoria, his mother grabbed for me.

Your hoodie looks good on me, no?

I send him the text and look at the time. At this hour, he would he walking toward the cafeteria for lunch probably talking with Austin. They would have just gotten out of chemistry together and are bound to complain about it to his each other. I start to put my phone back in my pocket when it dings.

As always, the reply says making me smile. I like his message and start heading to out of his room as the time starts getting closer to 11. I tuck my phone back in my pocket and his mom finds me. "That Oliver?", she nods toward the phone.

"Yeah, I was just letting him know I'm taking his hoodie", I say grabbing for one of the muffins on the table. His mom laughs,"You would think I would be doing extra laundry because of your clothes but then I find that Oliver has twice as many clothes?" I laugh along with her, starting to eat the muffin.

"Grab it to go, we've got to go", his dad appears in the kitchen. He heads to his wife, places a hand on her waist and plants a kiss on her lip. I manavuer away from them and toward the front door. I walk out and into his car, busy eating the muffin.

Are you leaving now?

Yeah waiting for your dad to finish making out with your mom

They've got to be stopped, his reply comes back making me laugh which is coincidently when his dad gets in the car. He glances at me with a raised eyebrow and I try not to laugh again.

He is here, I type back. His dad doesn't question my laughter and drives us to the hospital without talking.

□•□•□□•

"So that is medicine for the head pain, Sleeping medication, and some cream for your ribs?", his dad asks once we are in the office. The good thing about having Oliver's dad as a doctor is that he doesn't make me talk to another one and instead the process is so much faster and easier on me.

"Yeah", I say and he writes that down. A slow smile appears on his face and his face twinkles with mischief and I know he is about to say something bad.

"How about birth control?", I freaking knew it. My face flames so hot but he laughs. Throwing his head back he laughs so hard a few patients look over at us from their rooms. I pull out my phone and type: Your father just asked if I wanted to get prescribed birth control

No way, he types back making me nod through my blushing.

"Oh my God, that was too good", his dad says wiping at the corner of his eyes. I narrow my eyes at him and that sets him up again. He then stops, glances at me and says,"But if you do need it, just ask."

"God no", I say biting my lip and looking away. This has got so awkward. He stands up from his seat with a hand on my knee and I feel my heart stop. I close my eye against the sudden fear.

"Rory?", his voice pulls me out of my slight panic attack and when I open my eyes I fond that his hand has left my knee in no time.

"I'm sorry", he says to me and I shake my head. "No, I'm sorry. I didn't mean to."

"No, I know", I say and stand up to leave. "Wait are you going to drive me home?" The word home slips out of my mouth before I even catch it. I just referred to Oliver's house as my home. I guess it's true enough.

"When is your job interview?", he asks me instead.

"The lady said she had an open in at one thirty or right after school", I answering looking at my phone to make sure I have the correct answer.

"Can you wait here until one thirty then?", he asks looking at his watch like he has somewhere to go. "There is a conference room down the hall which isn't going to be used for the day. You can wait there till then and I'll take you to the job interview."

I glance at my phone, it's on eighty percent battery. I nod and he leads me toward the room. It is a fairly big room with windows so large but it is quiet in here. "If you need anything, call me", he says and leaves me to my own devices.

Chapter Twenty- Two

Aurora

After an excruciating three hours of waiting, Oliver's dad drops me off at the restaurant down the block from their house. I get in, feeling my heart beat pick up at the nerves passing through me. What do I say? As I approach the counter, the barista looks and her eyebrows deflate in relief, her shoulders slumping and I can hear her sigh from where I am standing.

She had been juggling taking orders and making coffee that the line was getting long and some customers started complaining out loud. "You're Aurora right? Get back here", she nods toward her and I walk to the back of the counter. She hands me an apron and says,"You take the orders and I'll make them." I nod chewing on my inner cheek.

"I thought I was here for an interview?", I say to her once the chaos of the afternoon rush ends. The girl, who I learned was named Jude, lets out a huge sigh as she sits up on the counter. I stay pressed on the wall.

"You were. But we have been so understaffed that I picked you as soon as you came in the shop", she says her blue eyes dropping to her phone that had dinged with a text when she was talking to me.

"Oh", I say not knowing whether to be happy or not. She types in a quick reply and then turns to me,"No but you were perfect. Poliet to the costumers and patient. I'm glad you walked in in the middle of a chaos."

"Okay", I say and she laughs. Her laugh is soft and easy. I wonder if she has a background of violence or if she had a nice childhood. I hope it's the latter. Costumers walk in and her laughter subsides. She hands me the notepad and the pen,"And we're back again."

I laugh and she smiles, grabbing her apron she dramatically took off a few minutes ago. The first costumer that approaches me is a old lady, probably the age of 70, wanting to buy hot chocolate for her grandbaby. It makes me smile and when I write down the order, I add a tiny heart. The next hour blurs by, eventful and stressful.

"That was crazy", I say a soft smile on my face when Jess tells me she has to clock out now. She clocks out and then turns to me,"Who is he?"

My eyebrows scrunch in confusion,"Sorry, who?"

"The reason you have a smile on your face at all times", she says pulling her brown hair up in a bun. She takes off the apron and hangs it up on the hook.

I only stare at her for a minute and she laughs. "I know there is one." I shrug and then tuck in a piece of hair behind my ear,"There is."

"Is he hot? Where did you meet him? Does he go to your school? How often do you see him?", she bombarded me with questions so rapidly, her eyebrows wiggling at each one, I only pick up on the last one.

"I kind of live with him", I say nervously and she glances at my face to my body, back and forth. "How old are you?", she asks and I laugh a little.

"I'm 17", I say.

"And you live with him? Your parents must be awesome", she says and I frown. I'm only living with him because one of them is dead and the other is abusive.

"It's kind of awful at home and his parents have been taking care of me", I say instead and she nods seeming embarassed at her earlier comment.

I wave off her apology,"It's kind of nice living with him. His parents let us sleep together last night."

"No wonder you are in such a good mood", she says and I shake my head violently. She laughs,"Even then. Tell me though, is he hot?" Just as I'm about to answer, the door rings at the notice of a costumer. I turn my head to find my boyfriend walking in with a huge smile on his face.

"Is my girlfriend employed?", he asks loud, his hands outstretched in obvious excitement. I walk out from behind the counter and make my way to him, falling into his outstretched arms. He tugs me close and I smile, happy to be in his arms again. He takes a deep breath in, smelling me and says,"You smell yummy."

"It's the shop", I answer and he sniffs me continuously like a little kid who walked into a candy shop. I laugh and then a clearing of throat makes me remember that we weren't alone. Jude looks at Oliver and then at me with an obvious smile,"I guees that would be an yes?"

"Definitely", I say biting my bottom lip. Jude laughs and then says,"Would you like something before I leave, pretty boy?" Oliver glances at her and then at me, raising an eyebrow. "Jude this is my boyfriend, Oliver."

"Oliver", she says going behind the counter,"Would you like anything?" Oliver smiles politely at her and says,"If you guys have a cinnamon roll, that would be nice." I put my hands together and walk behind the counter. "Say it again", I tell him and he walks up to the counter. He repeats his statement, only this time he is smiling wider and I write it down. I pass the notepad to Jude who rolls her eyes at us in a playful manner before grabbing a cinnamon roll and heating it up.

"This is kind of a look", Oliver says to me pointing toward my outfit. I laugh and say,"I got hired on the spot. Jude was so busy and due to being understaffed it was an easy process."

"Yup, only took a second", Jude says walking up and handing Oliver his cinnamon roll. He takes it from her and then pulls out some money. He hands me the two dollars which I ring up. This is an easy process. He grabs another dollar and says,"Can I leave a tip?"

"Of course", I say and point to the jar but Oliver has different ideas as he leans forward and places it in the picket of my apron. He pulls back, winking at me. I feel my cheeks warm but it easily subsides when Jude gags. It's funny how fast the both of us became fairly more than acquaintances. I look at her and she smiles,"Kidding. So you have school right?"

I nod and she continues,"So you can work only four hours a night. Come in as soon as you're done with school, and can you do Friday?"

I start to nod but then feel Oliver's hand on mine,"Oh no, I have to be at this ones basketball game but I'm free whenever."

"So that will be Tuesday,Wednesday, Thursday and Saturday", she says typing it on her phone. Then she adds,"And Saturday is going to be maximum of eight hours, would you want morning or afternoon shift?"

"Afternoon", I say and Jude types that in before looking up at me. "So, this is a rough draft but I'll have your actual schedule given next week. Remember to inform of expected absence a few days ealier so we can rearrange schedules."

"Okay", I say and walk over and take off my apron, placing it on the hook. She wipes her hand on her shirt and then says,"Well we are off. I'll see you Saturday then."

"See you then", I say to her and she offers me a final smile before heading out. I walk out from the counter and place the dollar Oliver gave me in the tip jar, before walking over to him. He immediately puts an arm around and says,"Let's go home, principessa."

I hum and he walks us out of the shop. "Are we walking?", I ask and he nods.

"It's only a minute walk", he adds and pulls me closer and we walk home.

□•□•□••□

"I don't know why you are complaining about this", I say to him the next day right after he came back from school. I had taken the day off again to feel better and it had worked. My head is feeling so much better today, it only hurt once. I'm glad my head didn't hurt too much this time but it makes as he didn't slam my head against the floor continuously this time. "I thought you would be happy about this."

I am dressed in a pair of my nicest jeans and a sweatshirt. I wore his jersey on top of that and thought that the jersey looked nice with a white sweatshirt. I also wore my hair up in a ponytail and had used an eyeliner to write out his number on my cheek. This is my official time going to his game as his girlfriend so I wanted to look the nicest I could.

Oliver grabs the hem of my jersey and says,"No I am. But I'm not sure it is a good idea for you to come to my name tonight considering your injury."

"I'm feeling better", I say to him, grabbing his hand and pulling him closer to me. He smiles and parts his legs for me to get in between them. I do and place my hands on either side of his face,"Now, we can sit here and argue or you can go on the court while I support you from the stands."

"The second one does sound better", he says leaning toward me. He uses a hand to slide it under my jaw, bringing my face close to him,"Only if you feel better."

I place my lips on his and say,"I am." My words are soft on his lips and he kisses me back. His kiss is gentle and yet I want more. I start to pull him in closer when I hear a voice behind me. I make a move to walk out of his legs, but he turns me around so I am leaning against them now. I retract my hands from his face, looking at his parents.

"Are you guys heading to the game?", his mom says while his dad looks away from us. We nod and she adds,"Maybe not try to make out when your parents are walking around, Nolan?"

"Maybe", he quips and I laugh, slapping his chest. I give his mother an apologetic smile and she shakes her head. "Kids", she mutters.

"Adults", Oliver says placing a hand on my waist and leading me out of the room.

"What do you mean, son?", his dad asks following us with his wife.

"Well you know, how you guys take every moment you have to make out. Upstairs and that's me lightly putting it", he says making me bite my cheek in order to not laugh. His parents have been very PDA, kissing every time they leave or everytime they see each other. I caught them making out on the couch a few days ago, his mom in his dad's lap, her hand snaking under his shirt.

Oliver just so happens to share this story to prove his point making me blush. "You saw that?", his mom says making it seem worse than I saw and I scrunch my eyebrows up in confusion.

"Saw what?"

"Oh", his mom says glancing at her husband.

"Disgusting", Oliver murmurs again and I shriek. "Bye we are taking separate cars." With that, he leads us toward his car and his parents walk to their car.

"My parents are disgusting", Oliver says.

"Disgustingly in love", I say getting in the car as he held the door open for me. I wait for him to come around the car and inside before I say,"I hope we are like that in the future."

"What?", he says genuinely confused.

"Happy to be next to each other alone twenty years into our marriage", I say and nods like he finally understands.

"Just got to marry me to find out, principessa", he said, starting the car.

"Maybe I will", I say, shocking the both of us before bursting out laughing. Oliver glances at me toward the end though, a smile on his face, his eyes evidently happy.

Chapter Twenty-Three

O liver

The opposing team is tougher than the rest, they have us running around like headless chickens. It shouldn't be this embarrassing but it is. And I've been feeling anxious knowing that this is my last season and if I want to get recruited, I need to be seen. I need our team to look good. So, when it is half-time, I head off the court and try not to grimace at the fact that we are 7 points behind. I hear the other team's laughter behind me but I make my way to the stands blocking the sound out.

I find my parents looking at me with worried eyes, I make my way to them and let them comfort me in their own way. And then I look at Aurora, who had been watching our encounter. It reminds me of the first week she came to watch me as my "girlfriend". She had looked at my parents and I and had frowned, I know now why that was.

"Aurora", I say slowly as I make my way to my girlfriend. She looks incredible in my jersey, her hair up showcasing her sharp features. She is strikingly gorgeous. She giggles as my hand makes its way on her waist and I pull her toward me. She squeals as I use my hold on her to hoist her up on her leg.

I don't give her a chance to respond when I place my lips on her; the kiss is short though. I lick my lips when I pull away and say,"New lipgloss?"

She nods, placing her hand behind her back and pulling it out of her pocket. She holds it out to me and I take it with a questioning eye. Strawberries, I realize that's the flavor. I look up at her and say,"We're losing, principessa."

Her lips downturn and she says,"I'm sorry, Oli. I know, I was on the edge of my seat." I smile at the fact that she was invested in watching me play.

"I'm stressed. I don't know how I'm supposed to beat them when they are this good", I whisper my eyes on her lip as I lean in and press the tube of the lipgloss. I place a finger under her lip and push it up, placing the product onto her lips. She looks down at me intrigued but I only apply it thoroughly onto her lip. I smile at how pretty and plump her lips look now. "Give me a bit of courage", I add closing the gloss and placing it on the small pocket of my shorts. Her eyes follow, frowning.

I pat it and say,"You'll get it back, soon enough." She frowns deeper and I squeeze her waist making her smile now instead. I lean toward her and say,"Got any advice?"

I watch as her eyes flash with something really quickly and her lips widen to a smile. She swerves so now her lips are close to my ears and says,"I can give you a reward though. After the game. Preferably in your room." My cheeks heat up at how suggestive her voice sounds. When she pulls away she has on a bright smile like she hadn't just whispered something dirty in my ear. I move my hand higher to her waist, just under her breasts and pull her in for a hug. Her hands go to my neck and I need to be even more closer to her.

Only, I can't because the marching band is winding down which means the game is about to start up again. "So, is the reward only for if I win, or an effort thing?", I whisper to her when she pulls away. She looks at me and her lips start to curve up,"Only if you win."

She throws me a wink that hits me straight to my stomach, making butterflies erupt. Only she could make me catch butterflies because in retrospect it sounds so childish, but it's true. I can't ignore the flutter in my stomach. With a final wave to her and my parents, I make my way back to the court just before the game starts again.

"That your girl?", his annoying voice pulls me away from my remincising of her whisper in my ear. I look to my right to find the captain of their team approaching me. Even though I'm not the captain, Austin is, he finds his way to annoy me every chance he gets. This time he chose Aurora as bait.

"Hope you weren't looking at her too hard, Creep", I say managing to not roll my eye. The name I used wasn't a nickname, the kid is actually named Nathan Creep; his parents set him up for that.

"She's pretty", he comments looking for her and I feel my insides churn at the unwanted compliment. He couldn't mean well with the way he was smirking toward her. "Maybe I'll take her home once I win." I don't realize I'm about to throw a punch at him until a hand takes away my fist that was inches away from hitting the jerk's face.

The way he spoke of girls was disgusting and I'm sure as hell not letting him talk about my girl like that. It was inhuman and disrespectful. Things she has already been exposed to so she doesn't need it from him as well. "Oli no", Austin's voice says from beside me. I retract my fist and instead put my hand in my pocket feeling the lipgloss of hers. It calms my racing heart down but I still glare at him. "Talk about her like that one more time and I'll make sure Austin isn't here to stop me", I spit at him my words coming in strong.

"He was talking about Rory?", Austin asks and I nod without looking at him, instead my eyes are zeroed in on the way the jerk smirks. "Really? Well I guess I'd have to help you out that time, bro."

"So that's her name", the ass of a teenaged man inquires and I'm about to throw hands again when the whistle blows signaling the start of the rest of the game. With a last look, I turn toward the coach and Austin heads over to his spot. Nathan stands beside me though and I whisper,"I'm winning tonight."

"We will see about that", he whispers back and I shake my head.

"Yeah we will", I say agreeing with the fact that he was going to see me win the game night, I had to because the girl whispering my name in the stands had promised me something and in return I plan on fulfilling that promise.

□•□•□•□•□□•

We won. Which is a big surprise as our side of the stadium kept cheering as we made hoops in. It was the kind of cheering just made me keep going. As soon as the timer buzzes for time, I head for my teammates in for a hug. Only three more games until we make it to regionals where we can start trying for state. The guys chant and I lose myself in the celebration, my voice becoming hoarse.

"Lose something?", a voice coming from behind me irks me. I turn around to see Nathan standing there with something in his hand. He holds it up and my eyes zero in on the lipgloss that was supposed to be in my pocket. "Need the gloss?", he teases his brown eyes playful.

I narrow my eyes and snatch the cosmetic item from his hand. A corner of my lip turns up when I say,"No but my girlfriend will when I kiss her in a short while." I leave him there dumbfounded while he watches my team celebrate. I head to the stands where I find my parents already making their way to me. My mom attacks me with a hug while my dad smiles widely.

"What a comeback. How many hoops was it, three?", he says and I shake my head with a smile. "Five", I hear a voice from behind him. My dad moves out of the way and in return I see my beautiful girlfriend standing there with a giant smile on her face. My mom released me from the hug and when I pass by my dad he gives me a pat on the back.

"We will see you home. Don't stay out too late", my dad says and I nod.

"I think we will grab food and then come straight home", I say really wanting to make my way to my Aurora. Instead I turn back to talk to my father respectfully. "No party tonight?", my dad asks and I shake my head.

"Aurora's not a fan of parties and I've been to many to know they aren't much fun", I say and with a final nod, I turn back to my girlfriend. She walks the distance between us and throws her arms over my shoulders. I lean down to return the hug, my hands on her hips.

"Let's get in my car. I want to kiss you really bad", I whisper in her ear and when I pull away, I find a small blush on the bridge of her nose. I graze my hand softly on her cheek and intertwine our hands together. I find the nearest exist and with her hand in mine, we make it to my car.

I don't even have a chance to buckle my seat belt when Aurora leans over and grabs my face in her hand. I grin as she places her lips onto mine, making me exhale in return. Her other hand makes its way to the other side of my face and I find her waist, pulling her toward me. Her kiss deepens and I tighten my hold on her waist to enjoy her. Enjoy this. She tastes good under my tongue and her lips are gentle even though the kiss is eager.

I'm smiling into the kiss when a car honks in front of us. "No PDA in the school parking lot", the voice none other than my best friend shouts. I release a hand on her waist and roll the window down. I throw my hand out the window and flip off my friend while my lips still move against hers. She makes a sound and I'm sad to have not enjoy it with Austin's laugh booming in the background.

She leans away shortly after that with a final peck on my cheek. "That was a nice game", she says once we have pulled out of the parking lot.

"Mcdonalds?", I ask her and she nods. "Thank you, principessa", I respond to her compliment. Hearing her say that I did good at a game is more exciting than hearing a crowd of fans cheer for every shot. It feels more intimate knowing thst the girl I'm in love with is proud of me. There is a bigger validation in that and I crave it.

"I had a little motivation", I say to her turning toward her to wink at her. Now it is her turn to blush at my words.

□•□•□•□•□•□

"Shhh", I say to her my hand on her waist as we make it up the stairs to my room. She keeps giggling at something we talked about in the parking lot while eating still. It was not that funny, but Aurora found it hilarious. It was a story of the first time I drank and invited a girl up to the roof to talk. While I was in the middle of acting hot, I had started slipping down the roof. The girl had luckily grabbed onto my hand and while I was in the middle of turning this into a heroic fantasy in my head, she had said, "Jesus you sound like a girl."

Aurora had burst out laughing at the line and had made me say the sentence again which promoted her to laugh harder. "Again", she would say with her hand on her belly her eyes already closed at the incoming laughter. I would say the sentence again but in a high pitch voice and that would send her off again. She hadn't stopped laughing and it's been thirty minutes.

The house had been quiet, beside a giggling Aurora, as we made our way into the house. My parents must've fallen asleep so we had to get upstairs quietly. Her giggling fit makes her hit her head on my door, which makes her laugh harder. I slipped my hand on top of her mouth, pushing her against the door, my other hand on the side of her face. She had slipped her eyes up to my eyes,swallowing.

I pulled my hand away from on top of her mouth and instead slid a finger onto her bottom lip. She had stopped laughing at once when my finger made contact with her lip. "You had promised me something if I won the game. And if my parents wake up I won't be able to get it. Now, come in quietly, principessa." I had whispered this and her had had flitted down to my lips at all times.

I moved away to walk into my room but abruptly turned around to her. "Fuck it. This is hot", I whispered before crashing my lips with hers, but my hand pushing her against the door. I wasted no time kissing her gently instead pushing my tongue between her teeth. she opened up and when our lips touched, it sent electricity through my body.

That caused me to want to feel her so I moved my hand from on her waist to under her crewneck. She tensed under my touch and I pulled away. My tongue made its way to my lip on impulse and she swallowed. My hands lay at my sides now and she glances at them,"I wanted to talk to you about that."

"About what?", I ask genuinely confused. She pushes herself off the door and me into the room with a finger on my chest. I try not to find it hot, but to no avail. Everything she does is kind hot. The word was probably invented for her. I watch as she closes my door behind her and I take a seat on the bed.

"Oliver you are really important to me", she starts making her way toward me. She takes a seat beside me and reaches for my hand. "These couple of months have been chaotic. But through the chaos you were there."

My heart starts beating fast at her words but I don't dare interrupt her. "Even though I was having a hard time at home, I was excited for the next day because I'd get to see you. I'd get to see your smile and feel the warmth spread through my body at the way your hands would slip through mine. It was weird, I'd never left like that with anyone else. You were the first person who saw me, truly me. And for some pecular reason, you stayed."

"I stayed because I instantly took a liking to you", I whisper.

She chuckles,"Which I don't even know why. Anyway, you showed me the light I was losing in my life. And when I truly lost it, you made me find my way. It's been a month since I've moved in to your house and honestly? I've never been happier, not for a long while anyway. I guess what I'm trying to say is..." she trails off but I really want to hear her remaining words so I squeeze her hand.

She looks into my eyes when she tucks in a peice of her hair behind her ear and says,"I love you, Oliver." My heart freezes at her words, she loves me?

"I love you. Ti amo", she says and my heart beat visibly picks up at the words. She really loves me.

Chapter Twenty-Four

Aurora

I told Oliver I loved him. And in return? He grabbed my waist with both of his hands and with what seemed to be no effort, pulled me into his lap. I straddled his hip, wrapping my legs around his torso. He pushed me up and guided my lips toward his own. I gently pressed my lips.to his and he put a hand under my jaw adding pressure to the kiss.

I want this to be memorable, so with a last nibble on his bottom lip, I pulled away. I looked up at him and say,"You heard me right?"

He grins widely, all his teeth showing,"I did, principessa. Why do you think I'm trying to kiss you?"

"Because-", I stumble on my words.

He presses his lips to mine,"I heard you. I love you too."

"I love you. God I love saying that", I say biting my bottom lip in happiness. Oliver looks at me like I'm someone who granted him his every wish, before pulling me closer and kissing me again. "Me too. Ti amo", he whispers above my lips before kissing me again. It made me giggle in egaerness. I guide his hand to my waist pulling my shirt over and letting him slip it under. His hands roam on my bare skin while I try to not make too much noise. But the noises make him kiss me harder though and I enjoy that.

"I love you", I whisper to him before placing my hand under the hem of his jersey and slipping my hand underneath his shirt feeling his muscles. He makes a noise which makes me kiss him harder.

"I could get used to this", he whispers and I push him down on the bed, laying on top of him.

□•□□•□•

I lay in bed shortly after our makeout session, Oliver had stopped after we had started touching his other as he was afraid to move things too fast. I understood that and thruthfully it was me groaning when his fingers made their way to the back of my bra to unclip it. He had pulled away immediately and instead started placing kisses on my stomach. Afterwards, he had kissed me on the head, told me he loved me, and fell asleep with a hand on my stomach.

I should get up and find my shirt, I think in my head but I'm afraid to get up and find my own bed where he would start showing up as soon as I closed my eyes. Here it was safe with the soft noise of Oliver's labored breathing. I loved to look at him the way the moonlight shone on his face, making him look ethereal. I wanted to stare at his face the whole night, but I was a guest in his house and his parents expected me to be in my own bed.

Especially after our makeout session, his parents would appreciate it more if I didn't sleep next to him. I wanted to respect them. I slowly picked up his hand and moved it off of my stomach, which was easy he had just fallen asleep. His eyes fluttered though and he mumbled, "Aurora?"

I placed a hand on my cleavage, covering it, "Oh sorry, I'm just heading back." I placed my hand on the bed and started searching for my shirt. He had helped me taken it off before, oh it hit me. He had thrown it on the floor. I made a move to leave in search of it, but his hand on mine stopped me. "Stay", he says.

I shake my head,"I can't. you're parents don't want me to, so I won't."

"Not even for me?", he says his eyes finding mine. He looked exhausted barely keeping his eye open. I sigh and lean down and say,"I love your parents too much to go against their wishes" before planting a kiss close to his ear.

"I love you", he says and starts to smile. I can't help but smile also. The phrase makes me feel warm and I truly believe I'm in love with him. "Ti amo", I whisper back and step away from the bed searching for my shirt. I find it close to the foot of the bed. With a hand still on my chest, I start to pull it over my head. My hand is still on my chest as I pull my arm through.

"Aurora?", I hear his whisper and pull it down my body faster. I look at him and he barely keeps his eyes open when saying," You're beautiful you know that? You don't have to hide from me. I love all of you."

I don't know what to say to such kind words. So instead I walk toward the bed once more and lean down and place a kiss on his lips. Even through his sleepiness he attempts to kiss me back. "You're so nice. Thank you, Oli." I whisper on his lips and then pull away. I leave his room with a smile on my face and that night I take the sleeping pill with the hope that it will work. I want to dream of happier things than him.

□•□•□•□•□

The next day, I have to leave the house before Oliver even wakes up because even though I have an afternoon shift, there had been yet another shortage of staff that Jude had called me in. I had a hunch that I would be working a lot of extra hours whenever I'm free. But the extra hours wasn't a complete downside, I was making 17 dollars an hour which didn't hurt my bank account. Frankie's Account, she left it to me right before leaving for Italy.

Find me when you graduate highschool, she had said to me last. I would find her and we would live together.

Work was instantly busy, me ringing up orders as soon as I stepped in. Jude was so stressed she kept taking deep breaths but eventually after two straight ours it began to die down. We stood and talked. Well I asked about her life and she shared that she was a first year student taking a few classes at community college. Money is tight for her so she is working every free hour to save up in hopes of transferring to an university.

I had assured her that she would be able to do it. She had asked about my college plans when I felt a hand on mine. I had flinched, my heart beating fast in my chest, but when I looked back at counter, I found the prettiest hazel eyes looking back at me. Oliver gave me an apologetic look at my flinching and then took the most dramatic breath I've heard anyone muster.

"I woke up this morning forgetting that you had gone to your room. And knowing you were already up at the time of 11 am, I headed downstairs in hopes of finding you. I looked in every room and imagine my suprise when I find my mom in the kitcen where she told me that you had work." He takes another breath at his rambling and then says,"You didn't even tell me."

I roll my eyes,"You were asleep."

"I would've been up in a second if it meant you were going to kiss me goodbye", he says and the thought makes me smile. Oliver had cherished our kisses so much and craved for them like I did.

"You guys are eighteen right?", a femeine voice pulls me out of my thoughts and I turn to Jude watching us with her back against a supply crate.

"I'm seventeen", I remind her. "Why?", I say and glance at Oliver who has taken both of my hands to hold them. Jude looks at our hands and then says,"You guys act like a married couple."

"No we don't", I ask her even though the thought puts a smile to my face.

"Yeah you do", she says and then glances at Oliver,"Waking up to kiss you goodbye? That's husband behavior if I've ever seen one."

Oliver visibly blushes making me giggle. The tips of his ears are red and theres a line of blush on his cheeks. Jude points at his face and says,"Never-mind. He is a teenager again." As soon as she says this, a group of teenagers walk in and Jude walks back of me to start preparing for me to take orders. I give Oliver a frown and he raises an eyebrow.

"Not getting rid of me", he says with a smirk. "I would like a iced caramel macchiato." I laugh but write that down and pass it to Jude. Oliver steps back and lets the other person order. Since we are short on staff, I get to hand hin his drink a few minutes later. When I hand it to him, he takes the drink as well as my hand and says,"I'm going to hang out with the guys. I should be back home when you are."

"Okay", I say softly. He leans down and presses his lips against mine gently. I want to melt into the kiss, but instead I pull away with a smile on my face. "See you at home?"

"Yeah", he says dropping my hand and grabbing the drink. He gets a napkin from the counter and heads toward the door. "I love you", he shouts right before leaving and I audibly sigh. I turn back and realize it wasn't me it, was the newly teenagers who are still staring at my boyfriend retreating.

"Where did you find him?", the brunnette one asks me and her friends nod along with her. "I want one", she says and Jude laughs from behind me.

"He found me watching his game", I say and the girls look at me like they are taking notes. I laugh and Jude joins in on me.

"He is hot", she mouths to me and I throw a straw at her. Oliver is definitely an attention getter but I love that about him: his confident demeanor.

◻•◻•◻•

Author's Notes: Less than ten chapters left guys, but I promise you they are good ones. They focus on their relationship and as well as a big plot twist.

Any guesses?

Chapter Twenty- Five

- -

A urora

The next day, Oliver's parents want to talk to me. Oliver and I had just come back from a date. Oliver had taken me to the aquarium where we saw tons of sea animals. It was so cute seeing Oliver get excited about his favorite animal which is a dolphin.

As soon as he saw sight of it, he pulled me through the hallway and toward the large ranks where they were placed. I laughed when he placed his hand on the glass and waited for one of them to float by. I laughed harder when one of them did making him grin so wide.

He had turned to me and said,"You saw that, right?" I had grinned giving him two thumbs up and he turned back to the dolphins, a smile on his face. I had taken a step closer to him and placed my hand in his jacket pocket, pulling him toward me. Placing my chin on his arm, I had said,"I feel like you are choosing dolphins over me." I pout playfully and feel his chuckle on my body.

"Never, principessa. I would always choose you", he says and my heart warmed at that. "Why?", I had aksed knowing the answer but hearing it from him made it all seem much more real. It also made me giggle, so there is that.

"Cuz I love you", he says simply before turning around and placing a gentle kiss on my lips. He pulls away and grins. "I love you so much."

"I love you too. Ti amo", I say always repeating the phrase in Italian for myself. Hearing myself say it in my native language makes it seem much more real. After that, we had spent the rest of the hour looking around for more cute animals and I had smiled at the fact this date meant more to him than me.

I loved the date, yes, but I loved the fact that he was so happy; seeing him happy made me happy.

"Nolan", his mother's voice had stopped us from heading upstairs. I move my hand away from his arm and instead place it into his hand. We had planned on sneaking upstairs to...well, I don't know. Kiss until one of us stops it from getting too far? Oliver turns us around and leads me from the hallway toward the living room.

"Mom", he says as soon as he sees her. His dad is also sitting by her, his hand in hers. That makes me happy, seeing his parents happy and together.

"How was the date?", she asks him and I realize by the seriousness from his father's face that this is just small talk until she said what she really called her son out here for.

Oliver squeezes my hand,"It was good. We got food after so we don't need—"

"We wanted to talk to Rory", his dad says cutting striaght to the chase. His mom slaps a playful hand on his father's chest and says,"Simon, we had a plan." He only offers her an apologetic smile and I feel my heart pick up. This had to be about my dad.

"I'm listening", I say softly my hand in Oliver's tightening. I take a seat on the couch and brace myself for what is to come. His mom glances at Simon one last time before saying,"You've been here for a month, so it has been a month since the incident. I think it's time for you to press charges."

I let out the breath I didn't know I was holding. My grip on Oliver's hand loosens and I let out a small chuckle,"I thought he would made an effort to force me back." His parents shake their head, looking at each other. I draw circles on the back of Oliver's hand and take a deep breath in.

"I'm ready", I say and his parents let out a sound of disbelief. "No, I've been waiting to. I needed my pain to simmer before wanting to press charges."

"Good, we can start the process now", she says and I feel my legs shake as I think of all the possibilities. What if I'm not ready when the trial starts? What if he spins the story and gets me back? I don't turn eighteen until a few days before graduation so that means I'll be stuck with him for another six months. I couldn't do it.

I feel a hand grab onto my leg making it stop moving up and down chronically. I look up to see Oliver smiling down at me. "Don't worry. My mother will find the best social worker if he doesn't get put in jail. He is not going to get you back in that house. I can promise you that."

"We", his dad changes the pronoun,"Can promise you that."

Victoria nods,"Yes, Rory, you are stuck with us from now on. We will keep you safe."

"You just have to trust us", Oliver whispers at me and I nod. His hand drops the one I'm holding and he slides the back of his hand across my cheek. I feel the wetness on my cheek then and feel a bit of fury at the fact that I shed a tear thinking about him. I had promised myself that I wouldn't think about him anymore, much less cry about it.

"It's okay, Aurora", he must've seen the look on my face if he had said that. I nod, looking down at my hand.

"So, what's the next step?"

Victoria smiles at me and I can see the pride in her eyes. No doubt she is proud of me. "We are going to go down to the police station and make a report. They are going to ask for a statement and you have to share as much as you can."

"Okay", I say when she finishes and looks at me with hopeful eyes. I glance at her hands and say,"But not today, okay? I want to remember today as the day Oliver took me out on my first official date, not the day my father would get arrested."

Maybe it's because of the atmosphere nobody seemed to catch the fact that I said my first date with Oliver when in their perspective we have been dating for close to three months. His mom nods and whispers something to her husband. I nod too and turn to Oliver. "Can we go upstairs? I want to take a nap with you."

He stands up and we start heading down toward the hallway. "Door open", his mom shouts back as we start walking up the stairs. Oliver chuckles as I hold in a grin, his mother is very strict about this topic but she should know that we would never go against her. Like, sure, we have touched each other but it was only the top half. She doesn't have anything to worry about.

As soon as we get in his room, I let out an exhausted sigh and hop onto his bed. I stretch my legs and cross my ankles before looking up at Oliver who has his signature thinking pose on: jaws locked and eyes forrowed. "What is it?", I ask him and he shakes his head looking at me. I watch as he climbs onto the bed next to me before asking again.

He looks at me then with his eyees so soft you would think he saw something sad. He sighs and says,"I'm just worried about you."

I place my hand on his stomach to reach for his hand, I intertwine our fingers together and say,"About what?"

He sighs once more and says,"I'm just worried about all that's to come. I know you can go through it but I don't want you to." And then he looks at me with a small smile on his face,"I kind of want to shield you from the whole world and keep you here next to me."

My heart melts at his words and I scoot closer to his chest. Leaning up on the bed, I place my head on the crook of his neck and take a deep breath in. He smells of sweet vanilla and a stronger husker decent I can't place. I do know that he smells good though, faint and that makes me want to be closer to him. I love that I'm probably one of the few people who can smell him, makes it more intimate.

"You know I love you?", I say into his neck and I feel his chin moving up and down my head. He pulls a hand over my waist and rests it there. We stay that way for a long time, and not long after I fall asleep.

In my dream, I see him waiting for me at the end of a flower field. He has a few in his hand and even though there are a lot of types of flowers surrounding me, the ones he has in his hand is glowing, calling for me. So naturally, I run toward it, toward him. I'm wearing a white sundress so flowly I have to keep a hand on my side to not flash anyone. I paired it with a white bow tied at the back of my hair which are in loose natural waves.

When I reach him, he holds out his hands so I run straight into his chest. "La mia principessa", he whispers in my hair taking a deep breath to smell me. I giggle as I pick up my head and say,"I love you, Oli."

"I love you so much more, Aurora", he says and I tkae notice of what he is wearing. He is also wearing matching white shirt with black dress pants. He hands me my flowers and starts leaving toward ne for a kiss. I immediately melt into the kiss but then hear my strangled breath and lean away.

I try drawing a deep breath in order to calm myself but there is something pressing into my neck making it difficult to breath. "Hello, Aurora", the voice says from behind me making the hair on the back of my neck rise. I remember that voice, the feeling of those hands.

"Oliver", I start to whisper but I watch him follow my distant laughter through the glowing forest when in reality he is walking farther away from me. "No, don't leave."

"Now it is just you and me, daughter", he had said and I had started to trash before another hand on my shoulder woke me up. I turned around to find the boy I loved looking at me with frantic eyes. Once he saw I was awake, his eyes softened and he said,"I'm here, Aurora. I'll always be here."

I moved toward him and placed a hand on the collar of his shirt,"You promise?" He leans up and presses a kiss on my forehead. I close my eye to savor the feeling of it. "I promise to always be here whenever you call, or ask me to be. I love you."

I let out a choked cry,"I love you so freaking much, Oliver. You saved me." He grins and I bury my head in his neck, seeking his comfort once more. He only tightened his hold on my waist and let me play with his soft silky hair. He felt good and he smelt good. God, I loved him.

The word I would use to describe Oliver is comfort. He is essentially comfortable and I crave him in every moment I'm feeling the opposite of it. He gives me the comfort I need to live. I'll always treasure that.

Chapter Twenty- Six

Aurora

Even with Oliver's hand in mine, my hand still shakes. He squeezes my hand to get it to stop and to calm my nerves but to no avail. Our hands shook as we walked into the police station with Oliver's parents. His mom had her serious face on, one I knew that meant that she was not going to let anyone step in her way.

When I looked at her, I imagined what it would be like to have my mother here. Victoria loved me and I wondered if my mom was here with me, watching over me. Victoria seemed to know me and understand me on a personal level; I didn't know anyone whose parents let them have their girlfriend live with them. I loved his parents to death.

"Hello, is there anything I can help you with?", the woman police officer asks me when we all stand up beside her counter.

I take a deep breath in and open my mouth to say something but I can't. All that comes out is silence. I clam my mouth shut and try again. This time I find my voice even though it is soft,"I'd like to file a report on my father." The police officer nods like this isn't a new occurrence for her.

"What for?", she says even though she goes to grab a pack of paper. I look at Victoria and Simon and they give me encouraging nods. When I look at Oliver, he gives me a nod and pulls our hands closer to his body. "You've got this", he mouths and I nod even though there is a lump at the back of my throat.

My voice comes out as hoarse as I'd thought,"For abuse." The police officer nods and says,"I'm sorry sweetie." She hands me the form she has filled out a little and says,"Fill that out. And we will go through with it at our next convenience."

I'm glad the statement I have to make is on paper so it isn't hard for me to say everything I need to. Even then, my hand shakes as I attempt to write down the basis of the abuse. Started when my mom died, became an alcoholic, got physical after half an year in, got sexual once my sister left for college. It isn't much to write but it takes me a good twenty minutes as I had to drop the pencil in the middle of filling it out to place both of my hands on my face in order to calm myself.

It didn't work nor did Oliver's hand on my back. He kept rubbing it back and forth and I tried to breathe but it was hard. But I needed to do this, for myself. So, I pulled myself together and wrote the rest of the statement. Oliver's mom, Victoria, helped me fill out the rest. My address and phone number. I hoped that they would arrest him as soon as they file this in.

Once we have everything done, I hand the form back to the police officer who offers me a sad smile. I avert my gaze from her pity. "Thank you for coming in. I hope everything goes well", she says to which Victoria and Simon respond with a thanks of their own. I, however, don't trust my voice so I just hold on to my boyfriend tighter. Oliver has been here with me the whole time and it helped me. Just a little but some nonetheless.

"grazie per avermi dato la forza, tesoro", I say to him as we start departing toward the exit of the building. He gives me a confused glance at my native language being thrown out.

I move closer to him even though his parents are walking ahead of their cars not seeming to hear us. "Thank you for giving me strength, babe", I translate in a whisper. His ears are a tint of pink and I know it's not from the cold mid December weather. He glances down at me and says,"It was in you the whole time. I only probably held up a flashlight for you to find it."

I smile at him and give his hand a squueze,"Thank you for helping me find it then."

"You're welcome, principessa", he says and plants a kiss on the back of my hand.

□••□□•□•

School has let out for the upcoming holidays and I am happy about it. It was hard to go to school when news of my father's arrest had been floating around the school. It was the biggest rumor at school and since kids were bored of exam season, they carried it along for an entire week.

The longest rumor we had spreading was only two days and that was when a couple got married. The rumor was true, the couple had but the speculations of why was the case in point. There were rumors that the parents of the couples were religipus so they forced them to get married when the girl had gotten pregant. This was back in sophomore year so it should've traveled longer, but it had abruptly ended on the second day.

My rumor, however, lasted the whole last week before break. Maybe it was because of the fact that I never stopped to address the rumors. Some people were sorry for me while others snickered like they haven't ever had sympathy in their life ever. Some even nade dirty jokes of my father and I and those are the ones that I cried hard about in Oliver's arms. How could people be so cruel?

When I had asked Oliver that he only had pressed a kiss to my temple and whispered,"I'm sorry, la mia principessa." My sobs had gotten louder then but Oliver had only held me tighter not once worried about me ruining his perfectly crisp t-shirt.

Now that school was let out and the both of us were going to be spending the full day with each other while his parents still had work the first couple of days, his parents made us go to the living room to have a talk. I had held onto Oliver's hand as we walked to the living room and when we sat down both his parents had glanced at it. Tucking in a piece of hair behind my ear, I looked down at the floor.

"So, Nolan", his dad starts, looking at his son. He turns to me,"Rory." The both of us give him a nod and his mom smiles warmly at us.

"Simon and I don't go on break until Christmas eve so that means the both of you will spend entire days alone", his mom starts making me glance at Oliver. "And I'm not going to play dumb and think that you guys aren't teenagers who have needs", she looks away from us and to the floor,"Sexual needs."

"Mom", Oliver shouts making a move to get off the couch. I had shouted her name too but stayed rooted in my spot. Oliver's dad extended a hand out and made his son sit back down. My cheeks had started flushing and no doubt I am red all over right now. Oliver's ears are red so that definetly means my whole face is red as well.

"Nolan, I know. And I'm not here to say that don't do it", his mom says and my eyebrows forrow in confusion.

"What?", Oliver voices my thoughts and his mother shakes her head. She turns around to her husband and he gives her a look. I watch in amusement as they silently fight before his dad frowns and his mom shimmies in her spot. I guess she has won evidently. I hold in a laugh and so does Oliver up until his dad starts speaking again.

Simon clears his throat,"What your mother failed", he says glancing at her in a mock glare,"To say was that we want you giys to be careful. so if you guys are doing." He stops and makes a weird gesture with both of his hands making me shriek and Oliver groan. "Things", he eventually says scratching his head and says,"We want you guys to be happy but we also want you guys to be cautious. So..."

"Oh my God", Oliver groans, getting up from the spot and says,"We get it, if we have sex use protection." His parents look at each other in 'why didn't we just lead with this' look and I bite my lip to not laugh. His parents are so overprotective but attempting to be uncool is funny. They wanted to be strict for this meeting but they can't even pretend to be. I smiled at the fact that Oliver had very nice and understanding parents.

Oliver leans down and offers me his hand which I gladly take. "Come on, Aurora, and don't worry parents, we aren't going to have sex." My cheeks heat up and I feel my face redden. Oliver had to make me blush harder by adding,"And if we did, we will use protection. I'm sure you guys bought some for me." I slap Oliver on the back but he only grins down at me.

I turn back to find his parents sitting there awestruck with their mouths hung open. Even though Oliver feigned typical teenaged boy grump attitude, his eyes soften and he says,"In all honesty, I'm glad you want us to be safe. So thanks for looking out for us."

His parents deflate and look at us with softened eyes when they nod. I laugh and Oliver turns to me,"And that is how it's done, Aurora." The sentence brings me back to something my older sister, frankie said. I miss her more now that he is in jail, I hope she will come back. I haven't told Oliver, but I pray for it every night.

Together we walk upstiars to our respective rooms to call it a night. I know that I don't have to be afraid to sleep in my bed because Oliver isn't too far away and if I need him, I can go to him. His door is always open to me. I love that about him, he wants me to be strong and independent but doesn't complain if I do need him.

□•□•□•□

The next day, I find that Oliver is overly excited as I enter the kitchen for breakfast. He had been cooking; not a surpsirse because occasionally he cooks. When I watch him from the doorway, I find that he is swaying his hips along whatever song he is hearing in his head.

"Oliver?" I say his name walking beside him. He flinches at the sound of his name in the quiet house and turns around to find me looking at him. I step closer and he snakes a hand around my waist pulling me toward his chest. "Morning", he barely whispered before placing his lips on mine. I start to lean toward it but he pulls away with a hand on my lip.

I look up at him through my eyelashes and watch as he turns off the stove that has a pan cooking scrambled eggs on it. "Wha–?", I'm interrupted when his hand in my waist is followed by another one and I feel my legs get pulled off the ground. My heart soars when he places me on the counter behind the stove. It is suddenly hot in the room and my heart is beating widely in my chest. Oliver's grin widens as he looks down at me, barely, I reach his height now almost. My feet are dangling off the ground and I watch as he slips into the space between them.

His hand moves off of my waist toward my jaw and he lightly runs a few circles with his finger close to my ear, making me shiver. Oliver had never been this hot before, since when did he get this hot? I feel my stomach dip. "Did you sleep well?", he asks me and I nod. He only moves his finger down my throat and lightly presses it making me release a sound. His grin tugs higher.

"Good", he whispers before connecting our lips again. I've been waiting for him to make the move so it's not a suprise when I straddle his torso and move closer to him, my chest pressed against his. I kiss him hard, wanting time even closer to him. He smiles against my lip and I slip my tongue in his mouth, suddenly thirsty for more taste of him. His tongue touched mine and he makes a sound of enjoyment that makes me slip my hand under his shirt. I trace the muscles on his torso, making him tense under my finger.

He pulls away from my lips to take a breath but it's not a while later when he pushes my waist down making me wrap my legs tighter around his torso. His lips meet my jaw, pressing hot kisses down my neck. He presses a few on my throat making me moan softly against him. He chuckles, a fan of the noise, and his lips start moving down my collarbone. I let him pull my top down to pepper kisses down my chest until eventually stopping at the top of my cleavage.

"Aurora", he whispers against me, still pressing kisses on my chest. I straighten my back to push up my chest and watch as a small smile pops up on his face. "Kiss me", I whisper and watch as his dimples show up at my request.

"Are you sure, principessa?", he says and I nod. His hand moves to my thigh pushing up the material of my shorts. He holds onto my thigh and I feel my heart beating wilder at this. His lips move down my chest and when they reach my breast, he sucks on the flesh making me moan louder. God, it feels good. How can he make me feel this good? I put one hand on the side of the counter and the other one goes down to his hair, pushing him down me. His tongue slips out his mouth and he runs it down my breast.

This time I calll out his name and feel him chuckling against my skin. He sucks the skin more making me hold on to his hair tighter. The hand on my thigh moves higher but he doesn't make any more move. Only up and down by making me press them tighter againg his torso. With a last kiss on my breast, he runs his tongue up my collarbone and toward my jaw. I can only look at him in awe. His tongue slips back in his mouth and instead he presses a kiss to my mouth.

"Holy shit", I say to him once he slips his hand under my waist and pulls me up. My hands find his neck and I pull myself up. "Was it suppsoed to be that hot?", I whisper in his ear, my breath coming in waves.

He grins, the dimples he has evident. "You liked it?", he says and I nod eagerly.

"I loved it. God you do so much to me", I say and he laughs. He moves his hip to mine and I almost moan again at the contact.

"You do so much more to me", he whispers and I can feel my heart still beating fast. I'm holding on to him tight as I don't trust myself right now. His hand snakes down to the top of my shirt and he pulls it down showing me. I look down to see a mark forming on top of my breast and he smiles at it. I only smile at that too, a little too hard.

"Do you want to eat breakfast now or–"

"Hold me for a few more minutes", I say interrupting him and pulling myself closer to his chest. I wrap my hands around his colder wne hide my head in his hair. "I love you, Amore mio." My love.

Once I feel my breath beat slow, I pull away and he smiles down at me. "Okay?", he whispers and I nod. He places his hand on my waist and pulls me down, planting my feet in the ground. I giggle when he makes no effort letting go of my completely.

"I made breakfast, principessa", he says soflty turning to the stove. "Though it may be cold by now." I place my hand under his shirt and move it up to his chest,"I don't mind." I feel him smile as he turns on the stove and grabs the spatula while I rest my head on his arm. He hums softly.

I could get used to this, holding him while he does any task. The need to be close to him and show him my love is strong. Loving him makes me strong.

Chapter Twenty- Seven

O liver

Ever since our makeout on the counter, it has been hard for me keep my thoughts clean. Whenever I look at her, my mind flashes with an image of me pushing her against the wall to kiss her. To own her. God, I've never been in love this strongly. Nothing compares to her.

Junior year I dated this girl, Jasmine, for a few months and I thought I was in love with her. We had fooled around a few times but I didn't have the thought of holding her all the time.

With Aurora, it's different. I feel the need to touch her, hug her, kiss her, but above all talk to her. I love talking to her because she listens inventively. I could be telling her a boring story of the dream I had last night and she has a hand tucked under her chin, making eye contact with me. I gotta say, I get a little flustered under her watch.

Aurora has been extra touchy with me recently too. Her hand slips under my shirt whenever we are alone and just last night she slipped it off of me to kiss my chest. Her hands hand traced my abs making me grind my hip up to hers. She had only bitten her bottom lip before leaning down and kissing it. Her lips touched every surface of my torso and then she chose a specific spot under my collar bone to torture me with. When she started sucking the flesh, I had made a noise that was far too loud for my sleeping parents.

She had only moved one of her hand up to my mouth and pressed down on it, continuing to torture me. Of course I enjoyed it, too freaking much. I felt like I was going to burst. She had opned her mouth and without even giving me a moment if notice, she had bitten the spot.

Oh my God. The moan I let out was shaky. "You taste so good", she murmured against my skin making her way up to my neck. I wanted to say that so did she but it got stuck in my throat. Her lips kept peppering kisses up my neck and toward my jaw. She sucked on the skin just underneath it and had whispered,"What if I left a hickey here?"

"Don't", I had whispered even though my voice was telling me otherwise. I really wanted her to. "My parents will definitely see that", I said and she had frowned. I placed my hand under her lip and traced the fullness of it. God, her lips were soft. I leaned up and pressed my lips to hers soflty.

"We have to go to sleep", I had whispered to her and she nodded but made no move to get off of me. I chuckled,"My parents can't find us like this in the morning." We were on the coach supposed to be watching a Christmas movie which we started but in the middle stalled watching as Aurora slipped her hand under my shirt. It was exhilarating and we were testing ourselves, just touching each other in the darkness only the tv illuminating light.

Now, I lay shirtless underneath her while she too has her shirt unbuttoned giving me a view of her chest and her toned abs. I wonder where she got those from, because the sight of them makes my mouth water. "I just want to be in your arms for a few more minutes", she says and I nodded tightening my hold on her. Aurora loves cuddling after makeout sessions and

I love them in comparison. The skin to skin contact makes the cuddling even better so I'm not complaining.

Afterwards, we had both sat up and I had got off the couch looking for my shirt while Aurora buttoned her shirt. This was pure love, wasn't it?, I thought looking at her now and then. I had seen her less the few days before Christmas as she had gotten extra shifts at work.

Now it was Christmas eve and my parents had cooked dinner which we were most likely going to eat tomorrow night as well. Both of my parents had watched a movie with us before heading upstairs to their room. They had been giggling and holding on to each other so I didn't even have to know a lot to know that they were going to be making out in no time. I hoped that that was it, though.

I looked over at Aurora and she had a frown on her face. I placed my hand behind her head and pulled her closer to me. "What's wrong, la mia principessa?" She had pulled up her knees to her chest and was now rocking softly against me. "What's wrong?", I asked again and when she looked at me I could tell that her eyes were watering.

"This is the first Christmas I'm spending without my family", she says and I tighten my hold on her. Her father had been in prison for the time being until the trial which isn't until early January. She wipes at her eye, "I mean I spent the last two hiding out in my room, but it's different you know?"

I didn't know but I had only nodded to show encouragement. "At least I had a father before, now it feels like I don't." She looks at me then I swear my heart breaks. She counts off on her fingers, "A mother? Died almost five years ago. A sister? Left to save herself. A dad? Became a peice of shit that..." she doesn't get to finish her sentence as a loud sob breaks through her. She shakes against my chest and I don't know what to do but comfort her.

I rub circles on her neck and say,"You've got me. My dad, my mom. You've got us."

"I know but–"

"The absence of your family is hitting you hard", I say for her to which she nods wiping her tears away. I place a gentle finger under her chin, making her looking up at me and say,"I'm sorry. I feel for you. My parents feel for you. We just want you to be happy."

She smiles a little,"I am happy here. Your parents are so nice, and caring. You are so sweet, taking me out on dates and loving me. I'm thankful for that, I'm just so sad."

"I'm sorry, Aurora", I say starting to get teary eyed at the fact that she is. "Wanna stay down here and fall asleep together?" My parents surely wouldn't have problem with the two of us on the couch.

Her eyes light up a little,"And we can wake up while the snow falls. Oh, Oliver, you have to open the curtians."

"I will", I say tucking a peice of hair behind her ear,"We will wake up in each others arms with the snow falling down. The house will smell like cinnamon and my parents will he dressed in Santa and Mrs. santa costumes sipping coffee. Everything will be alright tomorrow."

Her eyes soften and she closes her eyes, probably watching it all happen in her mind. When she opens her eyees she says,"You guys are now my family, right?"

"Damn right", I agree placing a kiss on her forehead.

□••□•□

When I wake up the next time, the both of us are laying on the couch together. My arm is lazily wrapped around her torso and her back is against my chest. Despite this couch, I slept good. I placed a kiss on her cheek and whispered,"Merry Christmas, Aurora." She had woke up and looked out our patio window, it was so big it doubled as a glass door. Outside it was white, and snow was falling heavily.

"Oliver, it's snowing", I can hear the smile in her voice. She loves snow, when it had snowed for the first time this year, we were in the car heading home from school. She had made me stop the car to get out and walk out to the snow. She had placed her hand out wide with a grin on her face. "Isn't the snow beautiful, amore?" I had nodded even though I was only focused on how the snow looked around her.

It illuniantd her pale face, making it brighter as well as redder. Her blonde hair fell off her shoulders in loose curls, so beautiful against the snow. The snow was falling slowly and she was catching them in gloves she bought for this occasion. She loved the snow.

Now, she was watching the snow in my house with a smile on her face. I placed an hand on her cheek and ran a finger down her cheekbones. She sniffled,"My mom loved the snow. She lived in a city where there weren't much, so her parents would drive to Turin every holiday to experience it all. She would've loved seeing this."

"I'm sure she would've loved being here with you, principessa", I say softly. The room started smelling more like cinnamon and we heard footsteps appraching us. I sat up on the couch as did Aurora as we found my parents walking in with a tray of cinnamon rolls in their costumes. They loved dressing up on Christmas morning for breakfast and gift opening and then spent the rest of the day in their pjs. It was a tradition.

So was walking in singing an awful Christmas song to say good Morning to me. I hadn't been able to warn Aurora so when she saw them singing a poor rendition of "Merry Christmas, Everyone" she glances at me with a horrified face. She giggles while I laugh at her. "You're parents are crazy."

I agree with her silently with a nod and my parents continue finishing off. They finish with a hand on their hips and a loud kiss on their lips. Aurora glances at me with another horrified face and this time I step closer to her and grab her face in my hands. She laughs and I smile at her. "Sorry", I mouth to her and she laughs hugging me now. I drop my hands off her face.

My parents look at us then and then at the couch. My mom drops the tray on the coffee table and says,"Did you guys sleep here?"

I'm about to answer when Aurora beats me to it. "Oliver thought we should sleep here since I wanted to wake up seeing snow." She sounds so much more appreciative with the idea and I smile not knowing it meant that much to her. I meant that much to her.

"Aw that was sweet of you, son", my dad says to which I thank him for. My mom claps her hands together and says,"Who is ready for present opening?"

We spend the rest of the morning opening presents and and squealing when my parents kiss. I give Aurora a necklace with a brown pendant which she requests I put on her immediately. "I'm keeping it on forever", she says to which I grin at. She had gifted me new hoodies for stealing all my old ones but I had laughed at that.

"You're welcome to steal these too", I say to her and she laughs. I love seeing her in my clothes anyway so I don't mind it at all. After all the morning fun, we all went upsets to get ready for sledding at a nearby park. Christmas day was so eventful and I'm glad that I got to take Aurora's mind off of the absence of her family.

I want Aurora to be content in her life, and I wish I could offer her that.

Chapter Twenty- Eight

A urora

Today is the day.

We have been at school for a week after break which means it's early January. I have a hearing about the trial this morning. Oliver's mom, Victoria, says that this meeting I won't see my father today but it doesn't help my nerves. It also doesn't help my nerves knowing Oliver cannot come this morning as he has extra practice because the season is ending and he has yet to get recruited.

He is extremely nervous, often times getting anxious even when I try kissing him to calm him down. When he is anxious, he gets too into his head making it difficult to convince him of anything else.

I used to be like that, too. But I am not anymore; not with Oliver at least. He is the one person that I always turn to. Whenever I am feeling a certain way, it is him who helps me out. Oliver isn't trying to shut me out in the battle of his own stress but he kind of is. I've been respecting him enough to not worry though. I'll give him space.

Anyways, Victoria is driving me to the court where I will meet my lawyer. I tried to get a government issued lawyer but Victoria said she had a friend who is very good at her job and that she should offer us less money. I hope that I can pay her in whole, my job offers about 340 every week, which is quiet a bit. I've been also taking extra shifts which helps out a lot.

I want to be financially stable once I graduate, to pay for college maybe even to buy an used car. Oliver promised to teach me to drive once the weather gets better so to not learn to drive in snow.

"She is a very nice woman", Victoria says as we walk into the courthouse. I've never been this afraid before, I wish I could call Oliver. He would know exactly what to say, but I needed to do this without him. I give her a tight lipped smile which makes her eyes soften. Pity, I recognize the feeling and I don't like it. But I guess that's what Victoria can feel for me at the moment.

I hold in a breath as she pushes open the door to a conference room where I meet the lawyer who will be hearing my case. My first thought is that she is beautiful with long red hair and bright blue eyes. She is dressed in a formal suit, the color green complimenting her hair. She smiles when she sees me and says,"Good Morning, my name is Natalia and you must be Aurora Moreno". She extends a hand out of my to shake.

I do so with shaky hands looking up at her,"Yes." She releases her hold on my hand and gestures for me to sit on the chair in front of her. She flips through her notepad and places her hands on the table, her demeanor calm where as my thoughts are so strong it is hard for me to sit still.

"Aurora, your case is fragile but not rare", she starts and I nod. "You're father could be tried with CPS but I understand you don't live with him anymore?"

I take a deep breath in and say,"Yes, the day he had made me pass out from the pain, I called my boyfriend."

"And his name is?", she asks ready to write it down on her notepad. I cross my legs together and say,"Oliver Nolan Baker."

"Okay", she nods writing it down. "Go on, sweetie."

"Right. He found me and took me out of the house. I never went back, only once to grab my clothes but even then I couldn't stay for long. I've been living with my boyfriend and his parents for over two months now."

"And that would be Victoria right?", she asks for confirmation.

"Yes, his mother."

"And since then, had you seen your dad again?", she asks me and I feel sweat bearing down my back.

"Yes", I breathe. "The day I went back for my stuff, when we were pulling out, I saw his car come up and he looked at me. I knew it then that he was going to come for me."

Victoria flinches behind me and says,"Why didn't you tell us?"

"Yes", Natalia glances at Oliver's mom and says,"Why didn't you warn anyone?"

"I was scared of even admitting to myself", I say my voice wavering. "He was my dad you know? He was the only only family I had left." I hated how a pathetic tear slipped down my cheek. "I didn't want to say anything as the next step would be filing a police report on him. I wasn't living with him and that was good enough."

"When was the next time you saw him?", she says writing something down. I take a deep breath in and say,"The last Monday of November. I was watching my boyfriend's basketball practice when I felt him beside me, I knew his breathing. In that moment, all that I've been fearing came true. He pinned my hands together and before I could scream he used his other hand to pull me away from the bleachers and underneath them instead, away from view.

He knew I was scared. He asked me where I was. But I knew he didn't care. He only wanted to punish me for going against him. I had found my voice to yell and he had punched me. Repeatedly. I called out for help, but nobody could hear us. He hit me again and again until I was leaning against the bleachers for support. He had raised his hand to hit me again when my boyfriend, Oliver, had stopped it. I had blinked and within that second Oliver had hit him back. He had to hit him a couple of times to stop him from heading for me. He eventually managed to make him fall down. I rememeber, even with him being on the ground and me being in my boyfriend's arms, he aimed to hurt me again– pulling my leg. But Oliver had knocked him out again and then threatening him."

Victoria gasps at the horrific story, I had forgotten that I hadn't told his parents of the details. They had known Oliver stopped it but didn't know that he had to fight back in order to do so. Natalia wrote that down and said,"Okay so since then you have never seen him?"

"Yes", I say and take a deep breath in. "I stayed in for the first couple of days, to heal and to hide."

"I'm sorry", Natalia says and then looks me at with a different look. "What's next?"

"I want him to go to prison for what he did. It wasn't just me, but older sister had gone through it too", I say mentioning Frankie for the first time.

"Your sister?"

"Yes, Francisca Moreno, she is three years older than me and as soon as she graduated she packed up and left for Italy where she had gone for school also", I say to which Natalia nodded.

"Would you say that after she left, things got harder for you?"

This is the question I was afraid of. This is where it got harder for me to respond to.

"Yes", I say picking at my nails,"When Frankie was here he only had slapped me around, barked at me for things, but as soon as she left..." I trial off not wanting to think about it, much less talk about it.

"Come one, baby, you've got this", Victoria whispers in my ear placing a gentle hand on my shoulder.

God, I want to breathe again without it hurting to inhale.

"After she left", I start up trying again,"He started yelling at me more, hitting me more. This is when he started being sexual."

"Sexual?", Natalia asked her pen stopping abruptly. I nodded,"He would comment on what I would wear, so I started wearing baggy clothes. His hand would linger in places they shouldn't. And whenever he got mad at me, he would touch me in those said places."

"How bad did it get?", she asked sitting up staighter in her seat.

"To the point where I locked myself in my room. I would wake up early to make his food, run upstairs and wait to go to school. After school, I would make his late lunch and run upstairs where I didn't come out until the next morning."

"Were you eating at this point?", she asked and I felt my stomach dip at the question.

"No, it was hard for me to go downstairs to fix myself things. At first, I got really hungry to the point of stomach ache. But later it got easier, my body stopped asking me for it."

Her face falls and when I look at Victoria her back is striaghtened. "Would you eat at school?", my lawyer asked and I shrugged.

"At first but then my appetite slowed. I stopped eating completly at school until Oliver had to feed me himself. He never asked questions but his unrelentless chiding for me to eat, made me get my appetite back."

Natalia smiles,"Hs sounds like a lovely young man."

"He is. He is the one person in the world who saw me. He stayed by my side even though I said no more than two words to him and he respected me to never touch me unless I was comfortable with him."

Victoria sheds a tear and I'm not sure which part she is crying at.

"Okay, so that's your statement and I'll present it to the judge. If all goes well, you wouldn't even need trial."

"Really?", I said getting up, a small smile spreading on my face. Natalia nods,"I think so. But if it does go to trial, you have nothing to worry about. Get your story straight and everything will fall into place."

"Thank you, Natalia", I say to which she nods at. She says a few words to Victoria before we are dismissed. I leave the room feeling exhausted and don't talk to Victitia the whole way home.

When we get home, we meet Oliver at the driveway. I get out of the car quickly running up to him and collapse into his arms and he holds me tight. "Did you tell them everythin?", he whispers.

"Yes", I answer back. He runs his hand through my hair, relaxing me, "That's my girl."

"How was practice?", I say to him and he chuckles.

"Don't want to talk about it, it was awful. God, am I going to play basket-ball again or is this it for me?", he says and I pull myslef out of his amrs to look at him.

"Yes you will, Oli. You are a great player, just keep applying to their schools and be open minded."

"I am, but...", he doesn't say anything more but grabs my hand and squeezes it. I lean toward him and say,"I believe we will get through this."

"I hope you are right, Aurora."

"I'm here for you, amore", I say to which he smiles. "Thank you, principessa."

Chapter Twenty- Nine

O liver

When I walk into Aurora's room, I find her behind the bed. I walk further to see that she is grabbing clothes from her drawer. I cross my hands over my chest and watch her. She grabs the clothes and puts them in her bag, I wonder where she is going.

Is she leaving me? That queatin really tests my vulnerability. She can't leave me, not this week. Not when the voices in my head have been getting so loud and the discouraging ones are so hard to get rid of. If I don't get scouted this week, basketball will not be in the cards for my future, and I really need it; it's the only true talent I have.

I take a seat on her bed and say,"Leaving me principessa?" My tone is light and friendly but what if she is planning on leaving. Her house is free now, maybe she wants to move back home. She tucks in a piece of hair behind her ear, and tucks the sleeping PJ I bought her the first day, into the bag. She looks up at me and I want to lean down and press a kiss to her overly plump lip.

"Oliver", she says her voice full of surprisement. I hum in response and she continues,"Jude invited me for a sleepover."

Jude, the girl that Aurora works with at the cafe. She is sweet to my girl and knows how to make her laugh. I like that she made a new friend. I nod and point to the bag,"For how long?"

"Hmm", she hums walking up to me and then placing her legs over my knee, taking a seat on my lap. I place a hand on her waist to steady her and she says,"Just for the weekend. I'll leave Friday night and be back Sunday afternoon."

"You're leaving me for two days?", I say feigning hurt, but it does make me a little sad. Aurora and I have been inseparable and I liked that.

"Why? Does that make you sad?", she says teasing me and I sit up straighter at her newfound confidence. Her hand trails up to the collar of my shirt.

"Of course. What are you planning to do for the two days?", I ask her.

"Well, Jude wants us to be ultimate sleepover. And then the next day she found us a spa place, which then we will spend the rest of the day getting our nails done and stuff. And then have another sleepover and then I'll be back", she says. That's a lot.

"Really?", I say my hand making its way up to her jaw. "And will you miss me?", I tease, but really wanted her to say yes. To say that she would miss me as much as I'd miss her.

She giggles, and the sound is a song to my ears, "Between sleepovers and the spa..." She trials off a smile edging on to her lips. She is playing with me and even then I feel a little hurt. She giggles louder and then says,"No, I'm kidding, amore."

Love, she calls me love and everytime she does it makes me want to kiss her. She makes me feel good her words and her accent when speaking italian. I linger at her every word regardless. I chuckle at her attempt at a great joke and say,"No, have fun with Jude. I'll be practicing for the scouts next week."

"Oliver, they will notice you, and if they don't they are going to notice your overly cheering girlfriend in the stands", she says and I laugh at her statement. She has been trying to reassure me about my basketball stresses but I've been in too in my head.

"Thank you", I whisper to her before pulling her in for a kiss. Her lips linger on mine and I take the initiative and kiss her harder. She smiles into the kiss and that prompts me to hold her closer to me, our chest together. I love the feel of her against me. I pull away with a soft nibble to her lips and place my forehead against hers.

"I love you", I say to her knowing that she will repeat the phrase to me, but in italian. I love it because she says it to me. Just me. When we are in public I whisper the phrase in italian too just so she is the only one who can comprehend it.

"I'm going to miss you, okay?", I admit and she chuckled. I feel her laughter vibrating agaist me.

"It's only for a few days. In the meantime focus on yourself okay?", she asks and I nod.

"I will."

□•□•□□••□

Aurora said that she wants to work out with me today before my game. Honestly, I am so tired of the stress that I took her up on the offer. Half an hour of laughing with Aurora can fix my mind, for the time being. She had stayed with me after school, so we both headed to the locker room straight after school. I had dropped her off at her one to drop off her own stuff and then she said she will find me.

And she did, she stood in front of me while I was lifting weights. I have gone up to 200 now, and this is the wieght that is comfortable for me but I hadn't had the mindset to add a few more. "Hello", she says, dropping a kiss down on my lips while I am laying on the machine. She looks cute with her blonde hair up in a ponytail that is so high and bouncy. She is wearing a black workout set that contrasts her palw skin tone perfectly.

Her stomach looks extra toned with the sports bra. She looked good and I swiped my tongue over my lips to control my thoughts. She glanced over at the bar and said,"Nice."

"Nice?", I question why she sounds nonchalant about it. She laughs and grabs her water bottle and takes a sip. I watch as the water falls down her lip and into her chest. God. I shake my head and do a few more reps. When I sit up, she is heading to me with a teasing smile on her face.

"Can you bench me?", she says her tone casual and I laugh.

"With one arm", I reply and before she has a moment to argue, I have her over my shoulder and drop her onto the bench press. I kneel down and sit in front of her, my back toward her. "Get on", I request and she giggles, sliding a leg over my shoulder and then placing her hand on my hair for balance before following with the other one. Now she sits on my shoulder and I hold onto her upper thigh— the bare skin under my hands makes my head spin for a second but I shake it off.

"Hold on tight, principessa", I warn her before standing up only to squat again. I follow the movement a few times before she says,"Got it." Her laughter through it all made it so worth it though. I laugh and go to sit her down, but she presses a kiss to my lips before leaving though. She is kissing me upside down I realized.

She giggles when she pulls away and says,"Close enough to my spiderman kiss."

"Huh", I say as she gets off of me. "Which spiderman am I?"

"Tom holland, definitely", she says with a grin. "He is the hottest." I laugh and grab a sip of her water, which she tries to push me off from.

"Are you saying I'm hot?", I question and she looks at me with an endearing look on her face. I wish she would stop looking at me like that because it reminds me of how vulnerble she is with me. What if I hurt her?

"Of course", she says,"I'm solely dating you for that reason." My jaw hangs open but not because of the statement but because of the wink she throws me. I felt it down to my toes— it was flawless. She laughs at my face and then walks toward the pull up station.

"I want to try this", she stands and then frowns at it. "My arms are weak."

"Are you planning on punching someone soon?", I question with a smirk and she gives me a look.

"When I attempted to hit my father, it never worked out. It was more like a friendly arm touch", she says and I frown. Walking over to her, I place my hand soflty on the bare skin of her waist. She looks down at me and I say,"You are not weak. He was a strong man hitting his daughter. That was his weakness. You're not weak."

"Thank you, amore", I smile at the nickname and she looks back up at the pull ups. "Help me up?", she questions and I nod. She positions her hand on the bar when I hold her thigh up, giving her a boost. She moves her body up and I press my head to her stomach, moving her thigh up as well. She laughs and starts flaying her legs around.

"Aurora", I laugh moving away and she hangs on the bar. I watch as she pulls up and smiles widely. "Oliver join me", she shouts and I smile at her laughter. She sounds so good, I could listen to her all day.

Even so, I follow her demand and put my hand up on the bar outside of hers. She laughs at me and then says,"Go." I do a pull up and so does so. Her smile is brighter than the sun when she accomplishes her goal.

"Good job", I tell her and she smiles brightly before her hand starts to slip. I watch the fear in her eyes and with her reflexes, she wraps her legs around my waist. I can feel her body weight transfer on to me and can see that she is not in fear of falling anymore.

"Try that again", I say softly and the both of us do a pull up. This feels intimate, I realize with her body pressed against mine. We do a few more before she says,"I want to get off." I have other plans though and do a pull up until I am higher up here. With my chin rested on the bar, I lean down and press a kiss on her lips. Her legs tighten around my waist and she kisses me harder.

I smile into the kiss and am about to go for more when a voice interrupts her.

"What the hell is going on here?", Austin says and very carefully I pull away from her and jump to the ground. I place my hands on her hips and pull her down as well.

"That was...", she whispers not being able to complete her sentence. I agree silently and turn to my best friend who is gaping at us. He glances at the bar and then at us, the steps following for a few moments.

I raise my eyebrow at him and he says,"Were you guys making out while doing pull ups?"

"No, I was giving my girlfriend a boost", I say and grin down at her. Her face is red from getting caught which makes me smile.

"A boost of what? Sexual energy?", Austin says earning himself a slap on the head by me. He squeals and says,"I'm sorry. I was just going to say that it was hot."

"Were you spying on us?", I ask my friend and he shrugs.

"Only came here when you guys started kissing and stayed for a second in silence becahse my head was trying to process what was happening." Aurora presses her head onto my arm and I feel her body vibrate in laughter. I chuckle as well and say,"Austin you need a girl."

"That I do", he agrees. Aurora picks her head up and inspects my friend fie a second and I feel a little jealous. I press my hand against her waist and she glances up at me with a raised eyebrow. I let it go and she turned to Austin once more.

"My friend Jude is looking for a guy", she says. Austin's eye open like it's Christmas morning and his mom had announced that it was present time.

"Really? Is she our age?", he asks and Aurora pulls out her phone.

"She is a year older, in college. But look", she extends her phone to him and he takes it from her. It was a photo I had taken of Jude and her working. Austin's ears are tinted a little red when he hands the phone back to my girlfriend.

"Does she like me?", he asks.

Aurora shrugs,"I'll mention you at our sleepover."

"Thank you, Rory", he says super eager and without a moments pause, he leans in and hugs Aurora. Her body stiffens but she doesn't flinch, which is a good thing. My girl is doing so good on her way to recovery; the thought makes me smile.

"Sorry", Austin whispers pulling away as quickly as he pulled in. Aurora only shakes her head and says,"It's fine. Maybe a little warning next time?"

"Of course", he says and then turns to me. "We have to go, coach was calling you. Getting prepped for the game."

I nod at him and turn to Aurora. I place a hand under her jaw and pull her toward me. I press a soft kiss to her ear and say,"First, proud of you. Second, I'll see you in the stands?" She nods in my hand and I press a kiss on her lips for a millisecond but that doesn't stop my friend from gagging.

"Shut up, Austin", the words aren't mine. They're my girlfriends and I laugh. She shakes her head and stands on her tiptoes before kissing me on the lips. She pulls away and says,"Win for me, yeah?"

"Definitely", I grin.

□•□•□••□•

She left a few hours ago, right after my basketball game and I came home in a bad mood. Our team had won once again but not with enough points. Scouts have emailed me within a week saying they wanted to meet me, and I've been anxiously waiting.

And tonight, I decided to focus on someone else than me as opposed to what I had told her earlier this week. I didn't need to worry about basketball tonight. Tonight I will help someone else close to me. My mom had told me that Aurora's case is a lost cause as she was able to find an escape before reporting her father. They don't see the severity of it all since Aurora was living with us, away from him.

And that he hadn't made an effort to come see her at my house. Aurora's statement about him attacking behind the school completly went through their heads as once again, it wasn't that severe.

The whole case made me upset. Was Aurora bleeding through her head not fucking enough? Was her not going to the hospital because she was terrified not enough? Was her trembling whenever somone, mostly Male, approaching her not enough? Her trauma is being overlooked.

The only person that can help review the case again is Frankie. Aurora's older sister who had gone through the same thing. If Frankie makes a statement against him proving Aurora's case, then they will give more thought to it.

Aurora doesn't know. My mom didn't want to tell her or else she would be so terrified and have nightmares again. Her nightmares had been so horrible to the point where she would wake up sobbing, looking for me. Even though I would sleep with her in my arms, she would still wake up trembling. It broke my heart to see her that way, so we won't tell her.

Not until I find Frankie.

I grab my laptop and pull up a new tab. I've been recently working on a college essay, in order to apply to schools in case sports isn't my way in. I search Frankie's full name: Francesca Moreno. Nothing shows up with her picture. I search our city's name behind her name.

Nothing pops up and I'm puzzled. How is she nowhere near the internet if she lived here all her life? I sigh deeply and pull the laptop closer to me. I type in her name and and type her graduating year. Once again, it's a loss cause and I'm about to throw the laptop down when I remember one more thing.

I search: Francisca Moreno, Italy

This time there are a lot of things that show up. The Moreno women in the year 2007 show up, where Aurora is a baby in her mother's arm while the other one is holding Frankie's hand. Frankie had red hair growing up, but through the pictures are hair had gotten lighter. I look at Aurora's hair to find that her hair has always been pale but with the years of growing up, it got darker.

I skim the photos for a long time. My Aurora had been clinging on to her mom from the ages 3-15, at 15 she started gravitating toward her sister more. I find them holding hands and hugging in a few photos. Who is posting these? I press on one of the pictures and it takes me straight to a facebook page. I skip the sign in request and browse as a guest. I find pictures starting from 2007, and when I press on the first pickrre of the Moreno women, I find that is captioned: The girls are back for the summer!

Oh, I remember now. Every summer they visited the country. I find some more pictures of Aurora's mom by herself. I scroll further to find her holding a woman around her age. It is captioned: Sorelle per sempre.

Since facebook doesn't translate that, I copy it and insert it to Google translate. I find that it says sisters forever. The Moreno women went back every summer to see their family. The photos stop abruptly with the last photo of Aurora's mom, Catalina Moreno, and it is captioned: My beautful Caty, gone but never forgotten.

I wipe my eye and then exist out of the page quick. That was too emotional, I went through all the pictures of the girls up until their mother died. I type in college at the end of the search and an article shows up.

Francesca Moreno offered full ride scholarship to University of Padua.

There is pride in my smile as I scroll through the page. It talks about her academic achievements and her mother's legacy here. She was given the scholarship as a condolence of her mother's death. It says her mother attended here too and donated every summer they came here. That's why she was offered the scholarship.

I rub my chin and feel the stubble on it. Aurora had kissed me quick and said that it irrated her skin, I'm going to shave it tomorrow morning. God, as I sit here thinking of Aurora with an article of her sister, I wonder if she has searched for her sister.

Why did she disappear and where is she? I'll have to go research on that too. I have to in order for Aurora's case to be even looked at again.

Chapter Thirty

Aurora

I have over estimated my confidence. I thought I was doing way better than I really was. When Jude pulled up into her driveway, I was so happy at the prospect of having my first ever sleepover. I had told her that much but when we went in, I felt a shiver run through.

Because there was a guy in the house, he had been sitting in the living room. He had looked at us as soon as we walked in and said,"Hey, sis." Jude's brother, but I thought he had been away at college.

Jude crosses her arm and says,"I thought you were up at University?" He shrugs and says,"God bored so decided to come home for the weekend."

He then looks at me and I feel my heartbeat thump fast in my chest. I can't sleep when there is a man in the house. I'd grown comfortable with Simon but that was only because he was Oliver's father and Oliver was home for me to seek when needed. Now, I didn't have Oliver. I felt my hand shake as I held onto the strap of my backpack.

"Who's this?", he says still looking at me. I avert my gaze and look at the couch instead. Jude says,"My friend. We are having a sleepover, so stay away."

"Done", he says putting his hand up. Jude grabs my hand and walks us to the kitchen where she drops off the pizza we picked up before getting here. I had called her before the game and asked her if she wanted to come watch. It was perfect and during the game, I pointed out my boyfriend's best friend trying not to make it obvious that Austin was interested in her.

"Oh, he is...", she trailed off and when I looked at her she had a tiny smile on her face. She caught me looking and gave me a shrug,"I like his hair." It was a general statement but I knew she was attracted to him. Which was perfect for the first part of my plan.

She opens the fridge and grabs two cans of soda, handing one to me. She gestures at the pizza, so I grab it and we walk upstairs. I hadn't truly taken a breath until she closes her bedroom door and dropped the soda on her dresser.

"What did you want to watch?", she asks me and I shrug. She shrugs as well and then picks up her remote to turn on the tv and scroll through a few movies. Eventually, she decides on Mean girls and I don't complain at the choice.

We sit on her bedroom floor and eat the pizza. We make commentry the whole way though. The ending credits start and the door to her bedroom door opens. I realize that she didn't lock her door and the person that pokes through head through is her brother.

"Jackson, get out of here", Jules yells throwing her empty can at his feet. He laughs and says,"I'm going to sleep, so don't make too much noise." And then he glances at me. I want to cower away and he gives me a tiny smile. I look away and hope that my hand isn't shaking as bad as my heart is beating. He leaves eventually with a insult thrown at Jude and I stand up on wobbly legs.

I grab for my phone, which is in my hoodie pocket. "What are you doing?", she asks me and I press onto his number. "I have to call my boyfriend."

She looks up at me and then says, "Okay, you can head to the bathroom. Right next to my door." I nod at her and walk out of her room, my phone already ringing. I head to the door close to her room but when I open it, it is evidently not a bathroom. It is bedroom and a guy takes off his shirt. God, it's her brother again.

He looks at me before I can close the door. He gives me a smile and I can feel that it is not meant to be polite, or am I being paranoid? "H–"

"Aurora", a voice syay from my phone and I take a deep breath in. It's Oliver.

I cover the mic on my phone and look at the guys feet and say,"Sorry, thought it was the bathroom." And then I close the door even though he was about to open his mouth to speak. I walk over to the other door and find that it is the bathroom. I get in and lock the door behind me.

"Oliver", my voice is a mess of unshed tears. I hate how weak I am.

"Principessa?", I hear him sitting up in bed.

"Oliver", I say again my hand shaking. I fist it up and say,"I can't stay here."

"Did something happpen?", he asks and I nod. "Oliver, I thought I was stronger than this, but I am not."

"Yes you are", he says and then says,"What happened?"

"Jude has a brother. And he wasn't supposed to be home but he is", I look in the mirror to find that my face is flushed.

"Did he try anything?", he says his voice rising and I shake my head.

"No, but I'm scared", I admit. "I'm scared. It triggered something in me."

"I'm sorry", he says and then says,"Do you want me to pick you up?"

"I don't know", I say and the realize how pathetic I sound. "What do you think I should do?"

"Firstly, take a deep breath. Can you do that for me, princepessa?"

I take a deep breath in and release it. I feel my heart beat calming down. "Okay", I say a little more calm now.

"Okay? Now, tell me, can you go through the night or do you want me to pick you up?"

I take a look around the bathroom. Jackson said he will stay out of our way and if Jude trusted him then so should I. "I'll stay", I say and my boyfriend appraises me.

"Good girl. Now if you do need me to pick you up, do not hesitate. Even if it's barely 5 in the morning", he says and I chuckle.

"Thank you, Oliver", I say.

"You're welcome, la mia principessa", he says and I feel my heart warm at his words. "You're a strong woman you know that?"

I didn't know it but if Oliver says it then I can try believing it. "Thank you."

"Okay, go in there and try your best. Have fun."

"Okay, amore. I love you", I say opening the bathroom door. I'm much calmer now when I walk to Jude's room. "I love you too, Aurora. Bye."

"Bye", I whisper to him and then hang up on him. I look up at Jude looking at me with frantic eyes,"What happend? Were you crying?"

I close the door behind me and say,"It's fine. Oliver took care of it."

"Can you tell me though? I feel like it was my fault", she says.

I shake my head and walk over to her bed where she is sitting at. I tuck a peice of hair behind my ear and say,"You know how I said I was living with Oliver?"

"Yeah", she says.

"Well the reason was because my dad was abusive and he hurt me so bad one time I couldn't go back", I start and her eyes soften. I chuckle,"But I'm fine now. I'm doing so much better. I don't flinch around people much but..."

"What?", she asks softly and I look away from her. She repeats the question and I take a breath in.

"I haven't lived with a man in a long time. Not one where I was comfortable with already. Oliver was an obvious and it took me a while to get comfortable around his dad, but then today I came here and when I saw your brother, well, the walls started caving in."

"Because of my brother?", she asks and I feel ashamed that I'm painting a bad picture of her brother to her.

"I knew that he would be sleeping under the same roof as us and I got scared. I was fine when we were in the room, but then he came in and relaize how easy it would be for him to get to me if we were alsleep."

"Rory", she says and I look down.

"No it wasn't just your brother. It was just a general reaction", I say and put my hand on hers,"But your brother is a good man right?"

"Yes he is two years older than me. He would never try anything", she says and I nod. "I'm sorry for..."

"No don't apologize for a trauma response", she says and I nod. "My brother is a good man but I'll lock our door if it makes you feel better."

"It would", I admit the pressure lifting off my chest. "Thank you", I say to her and she nods. She stands up and picks up a pillow,"Now are you ready to continue this party?"

"Yes", I laugh and before she gets to hit me with her pillow, I hit her first. She laughs out loud and I run away from her before she can attack me.

□•□•□•□•

"So, if you were older right now and had a career, would you marry Oliver?", Jude asks me as we are sitting on her floor. We spent the entire day out, getting brunch and then going to the spa she signed us up for. We also went to further get our nails and toes done, and the experience was worth the money. Afterwards, we went to the mall where we shopped a little before catching a movie. We were now eating takeout and watching yet another movie.

I turn to her and say,"What do you mean?" I knew what she meant I just wanted her to be more sure and for me to think more about my answer.

"Is he your great love, the one you would actually marry or is he just a teenage love?", she takes a sip of soda.

"Yes", I say too quickly and that makes the both of us burst out laughing. Jude holds on to her side and says,"Why?" I sober up at the question but with a smile I say,"Oliver is the greatest man I know. And I know that's a dumb thing to say at my age but I know that he would make a great husband."

"How?", she asks and I giggle at her asking all the questions.

I tuck in a peice of my hair,"Well let's see. He is incredibly protective of me, but in a sweet way. He is caring, so freaking caring. He is strong, both mentally and physically." I turn to her with a giant smile,"Wanna know a secret?"

"Oh my God, spill", she says as excited as me. I laugh and say,"So we were working out together on yesterday and I had teased him and asked if he could bench me and then—"

"No he didn't", she shouts loudly and I nod, my grin super wide.

"He did squats with me on his shoulders, I counted, guess how many?"

"Three?", she guesses.

"Seven", I shout and that sends us both laughing loudly. "And then guess what?", I say and that gathers her attention. "He kissed me while we were doing pull ups."

"How the heck?", she inquires and I bite my lip. This is one of me favorite memories with him. "So I had gotten on the pull up bar with his help right? Which when I say he was helping he was holding on to my body so I asked him to stop. And then he pulled away and then I did a pull up. I was so proud that I asked him to do it with me. So he got on the other side and our bodies were flushed at this point, but we did one. I was so excited but then I started slipping so I wrapped my legs around his torso."

"Omg", she shouts slapping my leg. Jude is a very abusive person when laughing. I push her away and say,"And so then he told me to do a pull up. By this point he was carrying me and there was no space between the both of us. None." At this the both of us squeal. "And then I was like let's get off and that's when he leaned down and kissed me."

"While you guys were on the pull up?"

"Yes", I shout and then say,"And we were going to kiss some more but his friend interrupted us."

"Stupid friend", she mutters.

"The one that has the "good hair", Jude", I say and that makes her look at me wierd. I laugh and she narrows her eyes at me.

"Why are you laughing?", she asks and I shrug. "Tell me", she says, batting my hand away when I go to grab my taco.

"Fine", I say and then grab my phone,"His name is Austin and well, I'm kind of working on setting you guys up", I say. I pull up a photo of Austin and Oliver and show it to her. They are both holding up a trophy from earlier this season. She inspects the photo before pushing it away.

"Why?", she asks even though her cheeks are reddening against her naturally tan skin.

"I told him about you", I say and she shrieks. "No, listen, I showed him a picture of you." She throws her pillow at me and I catch it. "The one where you said your jawline looked nice in."

That settles her down and she lets me continue. "And he liked you. I know he did."

"How do you know?", she asks and I clam my mouth shut. That's a whole line of privacy I'm crossing here. But she keeps looking at me and I blurt out,"His ears were red."

"He was blushing?", she shrieks and I nod. Austin's going to kill me, but this was a step in my genius idea. She looks away from me and grabs my phone, looking at the picture again. Her cheeks flush once more and I let out a whoop.

"Can you ask your boyfriend for his number?", she says surprising me but I only nod. I'd love to. I take my phone from her and text Oliver.

Can you send me Austin's number?

Why?, his instant reply makes Jude look up at me. I laugh and she smirks.

For my elaborate plan

Are you meddling?

Only because Austin asked me to

Aurora, he types and I laugh. But then he types back You're so funny. I love you, are you having fun?

Jude looks away from my phone at the fact that he wants to text more with me, but I reply back cutting off the conversation.

I am, I'll tell you about it when I get back

Tomorrow afternoon, right?

Yes, whenever we wake up. So the number?

Anything for you, principessa

I love you too!!!

He attaches the number after my last text and I look at Jude. She had been reading our texts and her lips are moving back and forth trying to figure out a word. I tap her hand with my finger and she looks up at me. "What does principessa mean?"

"Princess", I say suddenly getting shy. She only nods and gives me a 'I should've known' look. "It's Italian."

"He's Italian?", she asks and I shake my head.

"I am", I say and she nods. "Ahh, so he is calling you a nickname in which it is from your own native langauge. That's cute."

"Speaking of cute, I dare you to call Austin right now", I pull up the number and send it to her. She starts shaking her head but I keep nodding.

"Do it, come on. We can both have boyfriends who are in basketball", I say to her and that gets her to fold. She loves basketball players, she says she loves their height. I guess I do too, but I fell for Oliver who entirely different reasons.

Her hands shake as she presses onto the number and then pressing the green phone button. I move closer to her and the phone rings for a few seconds before Austin picks up.

"Hello", he says and Jude drops the phone. I look at her and she mouths, he sounds so hot. I laugh inaubily and hand her the phone.

"Hi", Jude says and I laugh at how squeaky her voice sounded. She pushes me out of the way and says,"Rory gave me your number but of course she had to get it from her boyfriend, Oliver. Your friend, right?"

I laugh once more at her rambling but Austin didn't seem to mind. "Jude", her name sets her cheeks flaming once more. I sit up straighter to hear this conversation. "Rory told me about you. How are you?"

"I'm good", she answers and I smile,"I was wondering if we could—"

"Come to my basketball game", he says interrupting her and she looks at me. I only nod at her and she says,"I was there yesterday but I will be next week."

"Okay, I'll pay for your ticket", he says and she shakes her head.

"No, I can do it."

"Then how would you be my date?", he asks her and Jude drops the phone once more. I laugh and pick it up for her, "Hey Austin."

"Rory", he says laughing.

"Jude says thank you and that she will see you later and that–", the mischievous look in my eyes gives me away and she slaps the hand out of my hand.

"Bye, Austin."

With that she hangs up on him and then turns to me. "You were going to say I loved him!"

"I was not", I shout back. I totally was but she didn't need to know that. I laugh and she joins in. Our laughter gets louder and then she says, "He is so hot, Rory."

I shurg and she fans herself. I laugh once more and can't help but think that this is a moment I could have with my sister. We always laughed together, added on to each others jokes until we couldn't breathe anymore. I miss that, I wish she would come back home. Maybe she will after my dad is in prison. I cling on to hope.

"I'd so marry him", she says and I laugh out loud. Our laughter is consistent throughout the whole night. I apologize to Oliver at 4am that I won't see him until late afternoon. We were definitely going to be sleeping in.

Jude is like a sister, her energy radiates warmth and I love being around her positivity.

□•□•□•

Author's Note: Hope we enjoyed the girl session. I'm sorry but next chapter....Let's just say I have something planned. I think there will be around 4 more chapters. Don't worry, there is a epilogue which will have both Aurora's and Oliver's POV.

Bye, friends (sorry, but everyone is my friend so...)

Chapter Thirty-One

O liver

I've been anxious this whole day. I woke up with a heavy heart because I realized that today was game day and that three scouts were coming to the game today. I had been groggily going through my classes and at the end of the day, my nail beds were bleeding from the anxious picking. Aurora, my sweet Aurora, had given me a bandage for the bleeding.

She leaned up and kissed me on the lips but I was so far away that she had sighed and pressed a kiss to my cheek instead. "Oliver?", she asked and I think I nodded. She looked so pretty. Her hair was in a super high voluminous ponytail with a streak of it temporarily dyed a dark green color. She is wearing my jersey and only my jersey. She paired that with a black mini skirt. My girl was hot.

I placed a hand on her face,"You'll be here with me the whole time right?"

"Front row seats", she says and I pulled her closer to me. I placed a finger on my neck and said,"Kiss me." She had only smirked and leaned in to kiss me. She felt good, she made me feel good. Her hand slipped under my jersey as she traced her finger up and down my muscles on my abdomen. It created goosebumps all over my body. Her teeth nibbled at the skin on my neck, over and over again and I held on to her as to not make a noise.

Only I did but she had nodded at that. God, she was hot. She pulled away too quickly and I had frowned. She placed her hand on my lip and said,"You have your game in a few minutes."

"I want to stay here. In your arms", I say and she smiles.

"I do too, but you've got three scouts to impress, go on out", she says and gets off my lap. I grab onto her hand and get up walking us out to the court. I release her hold on me with a last kiss on the lips.

"Wish me luck, principessa", I say and she gives me a huge grin which is the only luck I truly need.

"Good luck, Amore mio", the added possession makes me smile. "Thank you", I say quickly and the whistle blows signaling the attention of the audience. She walks away from me and I walk to the court. I find our coach giving us a pep talk and I hang on to his every word, taking all the advice I can get.

□•□□□•□••

We won the game, and yet no scouts waited to talk to me. One of them stopped to talk to Austin and I'm happy for him. I am so happy for him, but here I am holding a drink in my hand. Aurora had agreed to come to the party as it is the last one for the season. Post season starts next week and we are going to regionals.

"Maybe they will talk to you, then", Aurora is saying to me her hand around my arm. I lean into her touch,"Maybe." I take a swig of the drink and then go to grab another one. It takes me five minutes the finish the next one and I turned to Aurora.

"Wanna dance with me, sweet Aurora?", I asked her.

"Sure", she says, smiling at me. I can live in smile, I think. I'd like to live in it. I grab another drink and pull her to the dance floor where a lot of people are dancing flushed against each other. I pull her toward me and place a gentle hand on her waist.

"Aurora", I whisper to her and she scoots closer to me. Her chest is now flushed against mine and I look down at her chest displayed in front of me. She is wearing a tank top that shows off a little bit of cleavage with my Letterman jacket. She is covered but from this angle, I can see everything. I look up at her instead and she says, "Are you okay, Oliver?"

"Why wouldn't I be, principessa?", I ask her but I sound pathetic, my voice is barely above a whisper. She places her face on my chest and sways along with the music. "I'm sorry, amore", she whispers to me.

I only run a hand through her hair, over and over again. My heart hurts for her. "How can I break your heart again?" She looks up at me and I realize I spoke out loud. "Are you planning on breaking up with me?" She sounds sad and that makes me want to punish myself.

"What? No?", I could never think of breaking up with her. She is everything good that happened to me. Before her I was a guy with not as many qualities than I am now. Loving her made me a better person.

She takes my hand and pulls me toward the staircase where it is quiet. I don't want to have this conversation. "Then how else are you going to break my heart?", she whispers her eyes frantic. She knows something is wrong and I can't have her worry, not now, not yet. "Is it something with my father's case?"

I wish the two were related but they are not even in the ballpark of importance to her. I shake my head and she grows more frantic, her eyebrows downcast. "Tell me, Oliver."

"I can't. Not here. Not like this", I say and she shake her head.

"Then let's go home", she says,"I need to know what's eating at you."

"There's nothing eating at me", I reply back and she shakes her head.

"I've seen the way you acted the past week. Ever since I have been back from Jude's house, you touched me like it was your last. You held me tighter than you do usually. You told me you loved me about twenty times today, and that's only after school. What's wrong?"

"Can't I just appreciate my girlfriend?", I say trying to lighten the mood. She only frowns,"You helped me when I was at my worst. Let me help you now."

"I'm not telling you because I'm helping you", I say my voice getting louder. My head feels heavier and it's hard for me to look at one place.

"Oliver", she starts and then shifts away from me. "You're drunk."

"A little", I admit smiling a little. She moves further away from me and I have the sudden realization that she is scared of me. My Aurora is scared of me.

"Oliver", she warns when I try to touch her again.

"I've seen what alcohol does to people", this is a whisper, she is only talking to herself. "I want to go home", she says to me then and I move my hands away from her.

"Can you call my mom? I'm not feeling well and I don't want to scare you", I say and then say,"Aurora, I'd never hit you. Touch you if it's unwanted."

She looks at me and her eyes soften. "No, I know. But..."

"But you're scared", I say as she nods. I keep my distance from her and watch as she dials my mom's number. My mom picks up within a second and says,"Rory?"

"I want to come home", she says to her.

"What happened? Is Nolan with you?", my mom says and from where I'm standing, a good five feet from Aurora, I can hear the concern in her voice.

"Yes, we are fine. But Oliver is drunk and he has to tell me something and I just don't want to be here", she says and my heart breaks at her tone of worries.

"I'll be here in ten", my mom says and hangs up the phone. Aurora turns to me and her eyes soften once more,"You promise to not hit me?"

"I promise", I answer her and she doesn't waste a second before crossing the distance between us and into my chest. I exhale loudly and she wraps her hand around my torso, holding me tight. "I want to help you, Oliver. You have to tell me once you sober up okay?"

"Okay", I whisper, not knowing what exactly I'm agreeing to. I don't want to break her heart again.

"You promise to not hate me?"

"I can never hate you", she says and I really hope that she holds onto her words, her promise.

□•□•□•□•

Aurora wants to speak with me the minute I wake up the next day. Granted I woke up way later than her so she had been waiting for me to be up for a few hours. When I woke up, I found her sitting on my bed. As I looked at her, I think that she looks so vulnerable. She looks so peaceful and she trusts me fully and I don't want to break her.

"Tell me", she says when I sit up and stretch. I look at her and she says,"Tell me."

I know exactly what she is talking about but I feign forgetfulness so I can wake up. So I can gather my thoughts. "You said yesterday night you were going to."

"Come here", I say opening up my arms. She frowns but walks toward me and places an hand on my bare chest. She feels good, I wish we could stay like this forever.

"You want to know?", I ask her and pray for some reason that she says no and that she finds out some other waysand not from me becuase I can not bare to break her heart, be the reason she would feel awful. Those thoughts perish because Aurora nods and says,"Tell me what you were keeping from me."

I take a deep breath in and say,"Friday night I laid awake in bed but not because of basketball stress. But because there was something else, something I didn't tell you."

"My case not going any further", she says and I look at her confused. She sighs,"Your mom told me once I asked her."

"Yes and you know the reason. So I thought that there would be a way to help you."

"Oh Oliver", she says and I shake my head.

"No, so listen. I googled your sister because she could testify and with her statement, you had a chance."

"And?", she asks a hopeful glint in her eye. I feel tears rise up on my eye but I blink it away. "I found a lot of pictures. I found your mom, and you and Frankie", I try not to choke up. "You guys were so happy. You were so happy. You had a good life."

Her hands tighten around my neck and I go on,"Your mom was so pretty. Pretty like you. But that was it, after she died there were no more pictures."

With that statement, she lets a tear drop out of her eye. I wipe it away and she nods, burying her face in my chest. I place my hand on her arm to have her look at me again. "And I found your sister. She is beautiful and smart. She got into school for free."

"She did", Aurora chokes on her words. I look away from her and say,"She was. She was thriving in Italy for the first few months."

"She told me", Aurora says and I nod.

"But then she wasn't anymore."

Aurora only looks at me with that same hopeful look in her eye and I shake my head. "Tell me", she whispers and I close my eye. I can't bare to be the reason she sheds her next tears, I couldn't do it. But she deserved to know, she was counting on me to tell her the answer, so I took a deep breath in and said the four words that brought tears to her eyes instantly.

"She killed herself, Aurora."

Chapter Thirty- Two

A urora

My sister said that she was going to call me today; I went through the whole day with a small smile on my face. The guy I liked talked to me, it was a small conversation but a good one nonetheless. He is on the basketball team, not the captain but the other one. Not the blonde one with the buzz cut, but the other one, the one with the brown fluffy hair that grows every week.

When I saw him, I was walking toward him, my head down. But even then I saw his face, he had a smile on his face. There was hair on his chin that he was trying to grow, it was ridiculously adorable. When I passed him, I accidently bumped into him. He had apologized as soon as it happend and had kneeled down to grab my books for me. Our hands had accidently touched and I had flinched, not from fear but from the way I felt it down to my toes.

He had looked up at me,"Your eyes are so pretty", he said. I had almost began to cry and his smile tugged higher up his face. He was even more gorgeous up close.

"Thank you", I had said.

"What's your name?", he said and I shook my head. I stood up and he followed, handing me my book.

"Find me tomorrow and ask me then", I had said to him.

"I will", he said with a smile.

That had been our little conversation, lasted all of a minute but it replayed in my head for longer.

I got ready for the call, my sister was going to call me! She had promised me that much when she first landed in Italy; we didn't talk much. She was my best friend. As soon as my phone rang, I grabbed for it.

"Frankie!", I shouted at the phone happy to finally talk to her.

"It's Francisca, I want to be remembered by my given name. The name our mother gave me", her voice was deeper today, was she crying?

"Okay, Francisca. How's studying in Italy? Find a hot guy to obsess over yet?", I asked her trying to lighten the mood. She sounded sad before.

"Aurora?", her voice was impatient, her breathes coming in uneven.

"Are you okay?", I asked her grabbing onto my blanket. She didn't sound right, her voice was strained. "Can I see you?" Surely we could facetime.

"No, you don't want to see me now", she says and I forrowed my eyebrows in confusion. "Francisca, are you okay?" I asked again.

She sniffled, her breaths coming in more unevenly. She inhaled deeply through her nose and the noise I heard was anything but okay, was she sobbing? "Aurora you know I love you?"

"I do, and I love you so much more", I say to her.

"Good. Why did mom leave us?", she asks and the noises coming out of her are getting more worse. I wish I could call somebody but being this far away from her meant I couldn't do anything.

"She didn't leave us. She is still here. In our hearts", I say. I knew my sister wasn't fine, she was crying heavily. My sister never cried.

"She left us with him", and then she let out the loudest sob of all, and also a hiss,"God, I left you with him also."

"No, you didn't. I'm coming for you as soon as I can", I say to her. I loved my sister I could never think ill of her.

"I'm leaving you now", she says and with that my heartbeat skipped a beat. What did she mean?

"Frankie— Francisca, what are you talking about?", I say tears flowing out of my eyes. I hadn't even bothered to wipe them.

"I can't stay here. I thought coming to Italy was going to help, but it's worse here. I don't eat and I barely have a place to stay. And when I go out, I can't breathe. When did it become hard to breathe?", she says and I feel my heart hurt for her.

"Do you need help breathing, Francisca?", I asked her. Her sobs and hisses are louder in the phone and I get even more worried.

"I need to just hear your voice when taking my last breath."

"What do you mean?", I shouted getting off the bed. I was pacing up and down the length of my bed, my mind a mess. "Francisca, what can you see?"

"Blood, Aurora there is a lot of blood."

"Who hurt you?", I ask her. Maybe she got shot, surely she could get help there. I can send an ambulance, I don't know how but I'd make it work.

"Me", she says and I stop in my tracks. Me, she's hurting herself. "There's nothing keeping me here."

"I'm here", I whisper and she sobs louder.

"I know you are. But you're not physically here. I'm miles and miles away from you–"

"I can get on a plane right now", I have about 100 dollars saved up.

"By that time, I'll be gone."

The sob that I let out was the same as hers. We were one. I felt her pain and the pain of losing her all at once. I slid down to the floor, clutching my phone.

"Do you know the song?", she asks me and I nod.

"I do", I answer. "Francisca—"

"Sing the song with me", she says, her voice fading. "Sing it with me, please."

And so I sang the song with her in Italian until I couldn't hear her voice on the other line anymore. Francisca had died on the phone with me. There were water noises on the phone and I knew then and there that she had slit her wrists. I didn't know why she had left me though, and so I cried and cried, yelled and yelled, but nobody came.

Nobody came for me; I was now utterly alone.

□•□•□•□•

I remember now. I hadn't remembered before, but I had brought the awful memory back. I had brought the heavy hurt that I had buried two years ago back. And it hurt.

My chest felt as though it was going to fall off. I was holding onto Oliver but it wasn't enough. Tears were flowing out of my eyes so much. I was sobbing— no I was screaming. Nothing was coherent but I was screaming. This time people came for me. I heard their voices but it was blurred. The only thing I could hear was the song we were singing together.

fiorisei i miei fiori

Ti ho piantatoe poi ti ho visto sbocciare

così brillantepiù luminoso del solecosì coloratoi miei fiorisei così colorato

ti ameròfino alla fine dei tempi

ma anche allorasarai sempre qui

perché ti ho lasciatoquindi rimarrai radicatoil mio cuore

flowersyou are my flowers

I planted youand then I saw you blossom

so brilliantbrighter than the sunso colourfulmy flowersyou are so colorful

I will love youuntil the end of time

but even thenyou will always be here

because I planted youso you will stay groundedIn my heart Our mom had made up the short song and would sing it to us every chance she got. She showed us that she would be here with us at all times.

And my sister had taken her last breath on the last word of the song.

"Noo", I shouted the first word that was coherent. I felt him wrap his arms tighter around me but I got out of it. I was now attempting to hit him, but he had placed his hands on my elbows.

"No", I shouted louder now, as loud as my voice could go. He led me into his chest again but I didn't want comfort. I wanted to feel it all now.

I heard voices behind me and within a second, I was gone.

□•□□••□

"Aurora, can you hear me?", his voice was far away but loud. I could hear him; I nodded. "Oh thank god. My dad had sedated you", he had said and I sat up. I looked around and found that I was still in his bed. I looked at him, my beautiful love, he was in a shirt now but everything else about him was the same. He still had the kind eyes and the pretty smile. He was handsome.

"Why are you wearing a shirt?", I said sadly and that caused him to chuckle as well as two other familiar voices. I looked around to find his parents looking at me. I ignored them and held out my hands for my boyfriend. He came to me and I placed one of my my hands on his face.

"I remember now", I said and the three words caused me to let out an involuntary sob. He looked at me and I recognized that as it read that he didn't understand me at all. "Frankie died on the phone with me."

It made it seem all too real, I collapsed into his arm again. Only this time, I welcomed his arms; craved it. He let me sob into his arms for a long time, until eventually I looked up and saw his face. He was trying not to cry, it broke my heart.

"After it happened, I cried and yelled and sobbed so much. No one was here though. I eventually shut down and headed downstairs and drank my father's alcohol. Bottle after bottle. Until eventually I passed out."

"Oh my god", his mother said, placing her hand on her mouth and her husband held her.

"And when I woke up, I didn't remember. Even after I sobered up, my brain didn't want to remember. No one was here to remind me anyway", I say trying to stay calm but crying nonetheless.

"I'm so sorry, Aurora", the guy I love says and I nod. I place my hand in his and hold on tight.

"It was the day you first talked to me. You were walking with Austin when I bumped into you and you had stopped and knelt down to pick my books up. Our hands had touched, I can still remember how it felt to this day. Not then, but now it came back to me. You had looked at me and your eyes shined when you complimented my eyes. You asked me for my name and I said—"

"Find me tomorrow and ask me then", Oliver says, surprising me. "And I found you the next day. I walked up to you only for you to pass by me without a single glance."

"Why didn't you try again?", I asked even though I knew it was my own doing.

"I did, I tried for the entire week. But you kept passing by me like I was a complete stranger and then I didn't see you much after that", he says. "Moving on, Aurora, are you okay? How did she–"

"Die? She slit her wrists and then she called me and we sang until she took her last breath", I didn't mean to sound so bitter but I was. She died on the phone with me, making me live with the awful memory every day.

"We're so sorry, Rory", Victoria says and Simon nods along with her.

I only nodded at her condolences and pulled myself into Oliver's arms again. He was stiff under me and I looked up at him,"What's wrong?"

"I brought the memory back", he says and then looks down at his hands around my waist. I feel them loosen and frown. He starts to move away from me but I grab onto his hand.

"Stay", I say,"Please. I'm not one bit mad at you. I think I tried hitting you earlier but I'm not mad at you. I could never be", I say.

"You don't hate me?", he asks coming back to sit down on the bed. This time I climb onto his lap and place my hands on his face,"No, I love you. I love you, Oliver. So fucking much."

"I think we are going to leave now", I hear Simon's voice behind me and I turn to him. He holds his crying wife and I frown at her. "I'm sorry, Victoria. I didn't mean to make you cry."

"Nonesense, I'm crying for you. I'm so sorry, Rory", she says.

"Thank you", I say to her.

"We will be here if you need anything okay?", Simon says and I nod. Before they leave though, I say,"Can I get tylenol? My head hurts from all the crying."

"And the heartbreak", Victoria says but then nods. "We will have that for you, sweetheart."

"Thank you", I say to the both of them and they leave. I turn to the boy holding me up, without him I'd probably fall.

"I love you", I say to him and he smiles. His eyes don't have the same lightness to them they did before.

"I'm so sorry, Aurora. I love you too", he says and I nod. He places a kiss on top of my forehead. "I'm not going anywhere, Principessa."

"Good, you're not allowed to leave me", and with that I straddle him until he falls down on the bed. I press kisses onto his face. He chuckles under me and I giggle, but the lightness in my tone is gone too.

Gone with the memory of my sister dying. It was still hard for me to grasp onto, but I will grow used to it. After all, she was gone for two years now.

I had fallen asleep on top of Oliver before his parents had gotten me my tylenol. I was tired.

Chapter Thirty-Three

O liver

  She is laying down next to me, her long hair flowing down her shoulder. She is the definition of pretty and my heart tightens whenever I think about how much she is feeling right now. I know that, realistically, whatever I say or do will never heal her from what she heard.

What she felt. I could never understand how much she felt when her sister took her last breath. I keep trying to imagine it, I know she was shouting but how bad was it? Did she feel as though her heart was about to fall out? I'm sure she did; at least I know that's how I felt when hearing her.

The way she shouted when the memory came back to her scared me. She never had raised her voice and to hear the hoarse shout so let out made me want to hold her forever. She didn't want me to do that, she wanted to let her emotions out not be concealed from it. God knows she hid the truth from her brain for two years.

She went two years hiding the fact that her sister died, from herself. I could never understand that. The trauma response was so strong it shut out the memory.

I wish I let her hit me when she was shouting, maybe then she wouldn't be whimpering next to me. I wish that we let her express her emotions without sedating her. Maybe it's good that we sedated her, she woke up more calm. That's all we want from her, we want for her to feel okay, even for a little while.

That is why we lay half naked in bed. I had wanted her to feel good. She had smiled through a few kisses, but now her head is turned away from me, toward the wall, and I can feel her whimpers.

"Principessa", I say my voice low in the dark and quiet room. My parents had fallen asleep a while ago, but we were awake, our thoughts wild. She doesn't reply to me— maybe she didn't hear me because I spoke really soflty. I hold out a hand and lightly place it on her shoulder. She flinches and I hadn't seen her flinch that way for a while.

But when she turns around and sees me, her eyes soften and her lips curve up to a smile. The way she looks at me makes it seem as though I hung up the moon for her. I wish I could tell her I'm doing the bare minimum, and that she is the reason she is so strong.

"Amore", she whispers and I feel my heart clench at the tear that runs down to her ear.

"Are you going to be okay?", I ask and regret it in that moment. Of course she was, she is the strongest woman I knew.

She nodded, her blonde hair glowing in the dark and falling past her naked shoulders. I move her hair away from her shoulder and instead place my hand on her collarbone. I give it a little squeeze and she closes her eyes, savoring my touch. "I'm going to be fine."

I nod,"You know Frankie loved you?" She looks away from me and I move the hand up to her jaw, turning her around making her look at me. She does and there is pure sadness in her eyes, even the fake smile can't help it.

"Frankie was wrong for dying on the phone with you. For making you go through that, but I'm sure she didn't mean that."

"Then what did she mean?", she says another tear falling out of her eye. I wipe it away with my index finger and let my finger linger on her cheekbone. "She loved you the most in the world. She wanted to hear you while she took her last breath. She wanted you to be here with her." Aurora nods, taking in my words. She closes her eyes and I miss her green eyes. When she opens them, her eyes flash of anger.

"She put me through that. God, I was just turning sixteen. I had no one in the house, I was alone", her voice breaks and I can't do anyhting but run my hand down her cheekbone, hoping to calm her. She closes her eyes even so tears run out of her eye. When she opens them once more, her eyes are remorseful.

"God", she chokes out,"Am I horrible for being mad at her when she is dead?" I scoot close to her and wrap my arm aorund her. "You're not horrible for going through the stages of grief, Aurora. You're human."

She sniffles and places her head into my bare chest. Her body is pressed against mine, she is basically sleeping on top of me. "Thank you, amore mio", she says and I nod.

"I'm here for you", I say,"Anything you need."

She climbs on top of me to get a better look at my face. Once she is face-to-face with me and her legs are dangling between my thighs, she says,"I just want you to hold me."

"I will never let go", I say and then my eyes glance over to the door. "Aurora?"

"Hmm?", she is making herself comfortable on top of me, her breasts squashed onto my chest.

"We need to get dressed or else my parents are going to freak out", I say my cheeks warming at the thought.

"I don't want to", she groans and I chuckle. Reaching down the side of me bed, I feel for the shirt that Aurora took off me very slowly. I pick it up and hold it up, "I'll put it on you."

"Okay", she says her eyes barely open. She is on the brink of passing out. "Lift your arms, principessa." She does as she is told and I am granted a full display of her breasts. I try to look away even though I had them in my mouth not even ten minutes ago. I place the shirt over her arms and then when I pass it down her torso, my hand grazes her breast.

As if we didn't know that was going to happen.

I release my hand away from her and she opens her eyees to look at me. "Done?", she asks and I nod. She gives me a look and says,"What happened?"

I look away from her and she giggles. "Suddenly shy, amore?"

"Shut up, I'm a teenage boy with a horny mind", I whisper my cheeks heating up once more.

"Really? Is that so?", she says and when I look at her she is holding the hem of her shirt in an attempt to lift it up.

"Aurora", I whisper-shout and her laughter is loud enough to wake up my parents. I don't comment on it though because hearing her laugh is what I need from her.

I want her to be happy, and for now just in the moment, it is worth it.

□•□•□□••□

We are playing at semifinals today and I have a good feeling about it. This time Aurora was so busy hanging out with Jude that we didn't have a makeout session right before my game. Maybe that's a good thing because last week my parents saw the picures taken of me after the win online and I had a bright red hickey on my neck. They had the decency to not ask me about it, but I saw them giving each other a look.

I'm feeling good about this game because I saw four scouts walk in and one even smiled at me. He held out his paperclip board at me and my heart soared. He was here to see me. Austin was also in a good mood because just yesterday he and Jude were an official couple. Ever since, Aurora has been begging me for a double date with them. I told her what was the point and she had frowned. I gave in after a second so I had walked toward her and picked her up. She had dared to leave me with a frown on her face.

If my girl was leaving me, she would have a smile on her face.

The game was tough, I had started sweating five minutes into it. By second half I was drenched. But we were up by a few points so it kept me going. With half a minute to the clock, I dribbled the ball and waited for Austin to take his place. Once he was positioned, I dodged a few guys and passed the ball toward him. He had grabbed it and efficiently thrown it into the hoop, making us get a three pointer.

Aystin was a beast at shooting 3 pointers where as my talent lied where I passed or if I got lucky, made a dunk. Dunks were fun and with my height, it wasn't too much trouble. The crowd cheers so loud and I can hear my Aurora along with them. She is shouting my name and in Itlain saying she loved me. I loved her too.

I looked back at her and saw her jumping up and down on the stadium, her hair up in a signature sports day ponytail and my jersey on her torso. That's all she was wearing with tights underneath them, but my jersey was long enough to pass for a dress anyway. She looked like mine. I brought my hand to my lip and blew her a kiss. I heard her friend cheer loudly at that and I saw my girl blushing.

She shouted I love you again in Italian and I turned around to find Austin running straight for me. "One more game, bro. You think we can take the win?"

I look back at my cheering girlfriend and turn to him,"Hell yeah."

"That's what I'm talking about", he cheers and I laugh. He pulls me in for a hug and our celebration lasts for a long time. I feel the crowd die down and then turn around go find a guy with a clipboard heading for me. It's the guy that smiled at me!

"Congratulations, Mr. Baker", he says extending a hand toward me. I take his hand in a hand shake and hope that my hand isn't sweaty. "Thank you, Mr. Miller."

"Oh so you know who I am", he says and I laugh along with him. "I'm the coach for Davidson University, and I was wondering if I could convince you to join my team."

No way, I thought. It couldn't be this easy. The college that was an hour drive from here wasn't offering me a place on his team.

He laughs at the look on my face,"I've been watching you play for a while Mr. Baker. I heard about you a month ago, and last week I watched your game online."

"Oh, how did I do?", I ask, trying to stay modest.

"Not as well as this week", he says and I feel my cheeks warm at the compliment. I smile, and I can tell that it is very big. I can't help it— a coach is recruiting me.

"Thank you", I say and he beams up at me.

"I'd like for you to apply to our school", he starts.

"I did", I say way too quick. He grins like I made his job a hundred times easier.

"Perfect! So I'll take your full name to the admissions office and with your stats, you are a shoo in", he says and claps me on the back. I grin as well.

"Thank you, Mr. Miller."

"You can start calling me coach now", he says which makes me smile even harder now. Everything I've worked hard for is coming true now. He starts to leave but a thought enters my mind and I call him back.

"Can you look into another person who applied to your school?", I ask sheepishly.

"Is it another athlete? If it's Austin Reyes don't worry I'm going to him now", he says and I smile at the prospect of my friend getting recruited as well. The coach from last week hadn't offered him a position so it was good to hear that this one would like to.

I shake my head and run a hand through my hair. "It's my girlfriend. She has a 3.8 GPA and even though she hasn't been involved in school much, her essay is worth taking a look at."

"What's her name?", he asks and I watch as he picks up his pen to write it down. Biting back a grin, I say,"Aurora Moreno."

"I'll definetly talk to the admissions about her too", he says and I grin this time.

"Thank you", I say not being able to stay still anymore. I have to tell my girlfriend, she will be thrilled for me. I turn my head to find her walking toward me, a smile on her face.

Mr. Miller takes a look at her and then at my face. "Is that her?"

"Yes", I'm not being able to hold my grin back this time.

"Okay, I'm not going to waste any of your time. Just look out for an email okay?", he says and starts pulling away from me.

"I will", I say to him and he bids me goodbye with one last congratulations. Before he can even fully leave, I turn around to my girl and run straight to her. She giggles when I pick her up but I hold her tighter against me. I hoist her up and she wraps leg around my waist.

"Did he recruit you, amore mio?", she whispers in my ear and I nod twirling us around. She giggles louder and I crave to hear the sound at all times. With a tight squeeze I start to put her down on the floor. She laughs when her feet hits the ground and reaches for my neck.

"I'm so proud of you, Oliver!", she exclaims and I smile at her happiness.

"Thank you, Aurora", I say and she laughs once more. She stands up on her tiptoes and places a kiss on my lip. Earlier this evening she had refused because her red lip was going to transfer to my lips but now she doesn't seem to care. The kiss is too short though and she pulls away, but not without a wink.

I chuckle and watch my parents walk over to us. With a last touch to her hand I say,"It was Davidson University, he offered me a spot. And I told him about you."

She grins and gives my hand a squeeze. "What do you mean by the last part?", she says. My parents are standing right behind her now but I say,"I asked them to look at your application I along with mine."

"Why would you do that?", she asks.

"Definitely not for selfish reasons", I joke but then sober up and say,"No because you worked hard on your application."

"Thank you", she says keeping eye contact with me but then steps away to let my parents hug me. My mom hugs me first congratulating me and my father matches her enthusiasm.

Looking at my parents and Aurora standing beside me on the court, I couldn't help but think I had everything I ever wanted, and more.

Chapter Thirty-Four

- -

A^{urora}

"Isn't this so fun, Oliver?", I ask my boyfriend as we walk toward the restaurant where my best friend and her date is waiting for us. I've grown close to Jude ever since I stayed over at her house. Over the course of two months, she had been supportive and helped me through my grieving.

Nothing like Oliver though. Oliver stays in bed with me on the days where I feel the absence of my sister and my mom too strong, too heavy for me to bare. On the days where I am feeling like that, he stays with me in bed until I am ready to get even though he has his own plans. He holds my hand and when that gets too much for me, he silently supports me.

When I have my episodes of laying in bed, he buys me a book to keep me company. The first time he did that, I cried hard. He had been so confused to what triggered my reaction but I had only grabbed him and brought him to bed with me. I had held on to him tight and hoped that my gratitude was strong enough to convey a message.

The message that I loved him with all my heart. He is the reason I'm able to go through my day.

He had been there with me on the day the police officer released my father. He watched me sob hard at the fact that my father walked out free of charge. In the end, I hadn't been able to get justice. I did have a lot of support as his parents stood by me.

His father had told my dad that if he got anywhere near me, my father would lose a leg. He had sounded so serious that even I believed him. I did believe in his parents, believed that they could keep me save as long as I needed them to.

My eyes were narrowed in thin slits as I watched him interact with Simon. His expression was nuetral, his eyes blankly staring back at my boyfriend's father. My sobs has subsided and my hands itched for the door handle. I shouldn't do it, a voice said in my mind, but the other part, the part where I was his daughter, was louder. That voice told me to go on, so I opened the door and hopped out of the car ignoring my boyfriend's pleas to not do it.

I made my way toward him, my hands to my side. I didn't get that close though, but even then it was too much. Too scary. I avoided his eyes and instead looked back at Oliver who was following me. His mom stayed in the car, but I knew she was worried. But she restrained herself from coming out here, I had a feeling it was to protect herself. If she came out here, she would fight him herself. That wouldn't do anyone any good.

"Aurora", the voice I hadn't heard in four months said to me. I looked toward him, toward the father who gave me my eyes, and my heartbeat picked up. I placed my hand in Oliver's, without looking back, and said,"You don't have a right to use my name anymore."

That made my father flinch, he hadn't thought I'd come out here with my boyfriend to tell him off. He was expecting a weeping little girl who was too vulnerable to even speak.

He was wrong.

"Frankie died", I say to him. I wanted to see the look on his face when he relaized that his other daughter died. But the reaction never came even as I studied him hard. He only blinked once and looked at the ground as he said,"I know."

He knew? That didn't make sense, how the hell?

"I found you in your room. I had heard your screams from the car and I knew that something was wrong", he says.

I look at him, my father who knew my sister died. Who was there when I was screaming my heart out. Who made no effort in checking out what was wrong.

Oliver's hand in mine tightens and I say,"What?"

My father runs a hand through his hair and I almost flinch at the movement. I take a step back, hitting Oliver's chest, but my boyfriend doesn't make any move to step away. Instead, he places a hand on my waist, steadying me.

"I knew. I waited for you to calm down and then went inside to check", he says and I feel my blood pressure rise. He waited for his hysterical daughter to calm down before going up to check. "I found you in your room. The room was messed up, everything was broken. There were bottles on the floor, and then I saw the phone. It had cracks on it, but it still worked. I saw the call was from Frankie."

"No", I whisper but he ignores me and continues.

"I rang the phone again and a girl picked up, said that Frankie was gone", he says his voice not showing one hint of emotion. He was sick.

"Why didn't you tell me? Why didn't you want to talk to me? Why couldn't you forget your abusive side for one second to console your daughter?", I say and then added,"The only one you had left?"

That gets a reaction out of him. A vein on the side of his neck pulses and he says,"I did. I tried. You didn't remember."

"Why didn't you remind me?", I ask desperate to hear that he wasn't as horrible as I thought he was.

"You didn't know. If I told you, you would hurt."

"You were already fucking hurting me", my voice level is louder and Simon steps up. He says to my father,"You need to go."

My father steps back but I say,"No, tell me you felt something in that moment. Tell me you aren't a horrible monster. Tell me that the father who used to hug us every time he came home felt the absence of his daughter."

"Tell me", I pleaded. Tell me that you still care about me. Tell me that I'm not a burden. Tell me that you still loved me.

My father only blinks once,"I was protecting you. You didn't know, you wouldn't hurt", the second sentence makes me ball my fists up. "You want me to tell you that Frankie dying hurt me?", he finally amended.

"Yes", the word is barely a whisper on my lips.

"It didn't", he says and I feel my heart break, into a thousand different peices right in front of him even in Oliver's arms. "You girls were already dead to me, when your mother died."

The son of a bitch.

"Fuck you", I spit making him take back a step. "Nevermind, you are the awful person I've known you to be. I don't even know why I bothered."

I take a step back, pushing Oliver with me and turn around. Just before I take another step though, I turn around and say,"Just so you know, if you happen to make any move of coming for me, I'll find you first. You can't torture me anymore. I'm not a weak little girl anymore."

"Your---"

"No, you don't get to speak to me anymore. I'm not your burden anymore, I'm already dead to you. So spare yourself."

With that, I turned away. I shook off the way his eyes flinched at my words, I shook off his whole entire being. I walked to Oliver's parents cars and toward my newfound family.

The restraining order against him was strong, it gave me a little bit of courage to go out.

I never went out by myself though; I was too scared. I had Oliver with me or his mom, Victoria. Victoria was the closest thing I had to a mother. Her support and helpfulness meant the world to me.

"I never agreed to this", Oliver says and I grab his hand, intertwining our hands together. He is putting up a fight but he isn't lying. The only reason he agreed to me was because I had caught him at his championship last week, where he was so excited that he hadn't disagreed with me.

"But you did", I say feigning a pout and he laughs.

"I had to. You were too convincible", he says as we walk into the restaurant. Jude and Austin sit at a booth at the back of the restaurant and I let go of my boyfriend's hand to go toward them. Jude stands up when she sees me and I fall into her arms. She holds me tight and then pulls away, her hand still around my shoulder. She guides us to a side of the booth while Oliver sits on the opposite by his own friend.

"I'm so happy we're doing this", Jude says popping a fry in her mouth. They had already ordered, I look at Oliver and can tell that he is thinking what I was. We had gotten ready on time, me in a mini black dress and him in a dress shirt. But then he saw me and one thing led to another and suddenly we were both in bed and offically late. I had quickly zipped up my dress and gotten ready again having to do my makeup again. Where as, Oliver only had to wipe the lipstick off of his face and button a few buttons.

Oliver smirks at me and my body heats up. Jude glances at us and she bursts out laughing. "Oh my God, you guys totally made out before coming here. That's why we were late."

"We don't discuss what happens in the bedroom", Oliver says making it sound more worse than it really was. Jude laughs louder and Austin extends a hand toward her and into her own.

He leans forward,"See we could've been late too." Jude pushes his face away and says,"No way."

"Is a guy wrong for wanting to kiss her girl once in a while?", Austin questions and Jude and I share a glance.

"No", Omiver answers looking right at me. I slap his hand away and pick up the menu. His leg slides between mine and in return I slide the bottom of my heels up his leg. He glanced at me but I ignore him.

"You're going to kill me one day", he mutters shaking his head.

□□•□••□

The date was so much fun. I don't think I've laughed with Jude as much as I did on our double date. We had fun teasing the boys. We laughed so much and the guys pretended as they didn't care, but I knew they did. They smiled a little, at least Oliver did.

When we make it back home, it's odd that I call Oliver's house home but that much is true, Oliver's parents are waiting for us in the living room. Oliver's hand is at my back,"You think we can make it upstairs without them noticing?" I giggle and walk straight for his parents.

I walk toward his mom and plant a kiss on her cheek,"Hi." She beams at my affection and hugs me in return. "Hey, Simon", I say to Oliver's dad and he also beams at me. Oliver walks behind me and says,"You're making me look bad, principessa."

I laugh and he copies me by kissing his mom as well. I playfully roll my eyes when he says hello to his dad also. We take a seat on the couch and I say,"So I've been meaning to talk you guys."

"What about?", Victoria says while Oliver takes one of my hand, playing with the ring on my finger. I look up at his parents and say,"Future plans."

"Okay", Victoris says crossing her legs together.

"As you know I got accepted to Davidson University and I got a grant scholarship to cover tuition and housing for at least the first year", I say. They both nod and I say,"I plan on working while taking classes."

"That's fantastic. But you know we have money we can give you to pay for college", Simon says as I shake my head. I tuck a blond peice of hair behind my ear and say,"I'd like to pay for this on my own. Speaking of, I have money I want to give you."

Victoria starts shaking her head,"We can't accept that."

"But I want to", I say and she continues shaking her head.

"Save the money for college. You'll have to work less then, and you can always pay us back, even though we don't need it, later in life. When we both retire you can pay for our nursing home with Nolan", she says and I laugh.

"We'll probably invite you guys to live with us then send you off to a nursing home", I say to her and Oliver nods. He adores his parents and giving back to them is a goal of his.

His mom clasps her hand together, a dreamy look on her face while her husband pinches the bridge of his nose already knowing what's to come. "I can imagine waking up to a little toddler that Rory is cooking food for while Oliver is trying to get them settled for food."

"I've seen you've given much thought into this", my boyfriend says chuckling,"And anyway I think I'll be doing the cooking as I am not letting my child get food poisoning."

I slap a hand to his shoulder even though I am laughing. He has a point. "That's not funny."

Olivsr pulls me close to him,"Oh but it's true."

"No grandkids yet though okay?", Victoria says and Simon nkds agreeing with her. I shake my head and look at Oliver, whose cheeks are reddening.

"Not until after college", she adds and I nod looking away from her. The elder adults laugh at us and say,"Okay, we are heading up for bed."

I stand up too and grab Oliver as we head upstairs as well. I've been sleeping in Oliver's room for a month now and his parents have been notified of it, only under the circumstance of us keeping the door open. As if we would try anything with them in the house.

Oliver takes my hand and leads us to his room. I walk toward his closet and grab for a shirt of his to use as pajamas. This is a routine of ours. I head to the bathroom and am back after fifteen minjtes to find Oliver waiting for me on his bed. I hop in and under the blankets.

"I've been thinking of our future", he says to me and I nod. "Will we be together, say, in an year?"

"Of course", there is no hesitation in my voice. "Maybe there will be times where life is hard and we go on a little break, but I imagine that we will find our way back to each other."

"You promise?", he asks and I nod, leaning over to kiss him. Placing a hand under his jaw, I press a kiss to his lip, soft and lingering.

"I promise to always love you, amore mio", I whisper in between kisses.

He chuckles,"I promise to help you keep it, principessa."

"Through thick and thin", I whisper and meet our lips again in a much deeper kiss. Oliver and I are promised to each other and believe that we will be together forever.

□•□•••□

Author's Note: I'm crying; that was the last chapter. That was....God. it was a long one, I was dragging it out as to not say goodbye to my babies. They hold a special place in my heart.

BUT, one more part. Epilogue, I'm scared. I don't want to say goodbye (even though I already have it typed).

See you then!!

Epilogue

A urora

My boyfriend wouldn't tell us where we were going. He hadn't even let me check our tickets, instead hiding it for his own. It was hard for him to hide it from me when we got to the airport though. He started leading us toward the gate and when I looked up at the screen, I saw the location we were headed.

South Carolina to Italy

With my mouth obviously hung open, I turned to him. He had a cheshire grin on his face, his hands in his pockets. I looked back on the screen and blinked a few times to make sure that I was seeing correctly. There it was, my home country looking back at me. I hadn't been there in almost a decade, and the longing of going back makes my eyes water.

But I will not cry, I didn't need to. Instead, I took the remaining steps between us and placed both of my hands on either side of his face. He brought his face down and placed a kiss on his lip. This kiss was short but I was thanking him through it. I was grinning hard when I leaned back, my hands still on his jaw. "Oliver, amore mio, how did you...", I trail off the idea of it being so surreal for me.

"I've had the money for a while. I just didn't have the time. But with the sports team recruiting me and winter break falling perfectly on time, I thought I'd take my girl out to celebrate", he says as if the idea of him being so incredibly nice was just a causal after thought.

"Oli, what?", I say giggling. Oliver and I were on our last years of University. He had been studying business as well as playing for the college basketball team. I was studying real estate as well as social work. I didn't know which career field I was going into, so I'm doing a few more years of school to get degree in both. Oliver's mom and dad, Victoria and Simon, wanted to pay for my tuition but I hadn't let them.

Not one more dollar.

They had done enough for me: taking me in a quarter into senior year and taking care of me without even a single after thought. His parents didn't even let me clean the house as a gift to them, but I secretly woke up ealier on Sundays to beat Victoria to it. On Saturday, Oliver makes me stay in bed with him all day where we lazily watch modern family and, well, you can imagine the rest.

I worked at the campus stores, which wasn't much. On the weekends, Oliver and I drove down to his parents house where I picked up shifts at my old workplace. Jude had also transferred to Davidson University, claiming that it was for the better studies, but we all knew it was because of her boyfriend, Austin. Austin had also gotten recruited by the same pro basketball team and I couldn't smile more at the concidence. The two men were not going to get separated, and the universe would make sure of it.

"It's for you, Aurora", he says and I feel my smile widen. Throwing my arm around his shoulder, he crouches down and I giggle into his chest. I feel him chuckle underneath me and I savor the feeling. I savor every feeling with Oliver.

"Oliver, I love you so much", I shouted, wanting to hug him again. But we hear our flight being called, and in a hasty movement, Oliver grabs my hand and pulls us toward boarding area. I looked toward him and my heart clenched in my chest. I couldn't believe we were heading to Italy.

□•□•□•□□•

I watch as the snow falls down the big open window. It is dark but the snow lights up the whole apartment. I love the snow, it reminds of the two family members I have loved and lost. I wish to everything that they could be here with me.

Oliver's hand traces the shape of my left breast and I turn to him. He is staring at me openly, his eyes full of lust. I've known Oliver for a long time to know that it doubles as love. I slap his hand away,"Hungry for more?"

"Why? Are you offering?", he grins widely and makes a point to pull down the sheet I have wrapped around my naked body. I shriek and pull away but he only smirks at the challenge, leaning toward me until he is fully on top of me.

As I look up at the lightness in his eyes and the easy smile on his face, I think of how lucky I got.

It's been a few hours since we arrived in Italy. We had dinner at the rastruant down the block and then hurried to the hotel we are staying in. Oliver had only modeesly shrugged when I got overly excited about the large windows. He knew how much I enjoyed gazing out at the window while it snowed.

I reached up my hand and pushed away a lock of wavy hair off his forehead. His hair had grown longer since the last time he cut it, which was early summer. I loved his long hair though, it suited him better. "I love you", I mouth to him, not trusting myself to not cry at my overfilled joy. He grins, showing all his teeth,"I love you more, la mia principessa."

"Come here", I say, giving in to the attempted resistance of not wanting Oliver. I'll always want Oliver. I place my hand under his jaw and pull him toward my lip. He grins into the kiss and I shut him up by flipping him underneath me. I run my manicured finger down his well muscled chest and let out a small sound. "My turn, amore", I say and connect my lips with the skin at the base of his collarbone.

□•□□•□•

We are at breakfast the next day when I feel his eyes behind me. Oliver had always a point of making eye contact with me so I knew when he wasn't. And I knew he wasn't now unless he was staring at my hair. I had cut my hair at the beginning on college, but now it had grown to its original lenght. Oliver prefers it that way and honestly I missed my hair. I missed the way it made me feel, so I am keeping it.

Pushing a lock of it away, I groan and say,"What is more interesting than the girl sitting in front of you?"

"Nothing", he answered, still not looking at me. I grow tired and turn in my seat where I find a car parked close to the restaurant. The backdoor opens and a woman with dark brown hair walks out. My heart immediately lightens at the sight of his mother, but it only intensifies at his father walking out.

They both turn around, grab each other's hand, and turn to us. Victoria's face breaks out into a grin and she doesn't give her husband a warning before running off toward me. It's odd, she is running toward me, instead of her son. Even so, I get out of my seat and rush toward her. She pulls me into a hug and holds me tight. Her hand runs down the lenght of my arm until it finds my hand.

She feels my hand for a second before pulling away. She looks at Oliver and places a hand on her chest. "Good, I thought you would do it without us there", she says breathing like she is relieved. I look at Oliver and he gives his mother a stern look.

"Oliver?", I question and he turns to me, a big grin on his face. "Surprise, I invited my parents."

"What was she talking about?", I ask but Oliver ignores me, grabbing my hand.

"Come on, we have to book a room for Jude and Austin as they have of course forgotten to do so", he says and my jaw opens.

"They are not coming here also?", I ask with a hand on my heart. He grins and nods,"Oh but they are."

"Oliver", I say suddenly giddy. I lean toward him and reach for his arm, taking it.

"You're the best", I say to him and he grins. "I know", he says and then winks at his mom. His dad laughs along with his mom and I sense that I am missing something.

□•□□•□•

The following night, Oliver wants to throw a get together for his parents and our best friends. I tell him that Christmas is in a week so we should save it for later, but he persists. Even when I bribe him with the long nights in. I'm sulking when I walk out of the bathroom in a white mini dress. Oliver had bought it for me for this trip.

"Oliver, couldn't it just be the two of us tonight?", I complain as I walk up to him. He is also getting ready in the bedroom, buttoning up his shirt. I undo those buttons and say,"Alone, all night." I stand in the space between his legs and press my hand to his chest.

"Does that not interest you?", I whisper. He looks down at me, his eyes shining and I feel as though I'm going to take the win. He places his hands on either side of my waist and then, I can't even believe it.

He picks me up and puts me in a spot away from him. The frown is evident on my face and I watch as he turns to me,"Trust me, you will be more interested after tonight."

"What?", I ask him but there is a knock on door that pulls his attention from me. He walks toward the front door and pulls open the door, his fingers hurrying to button up the ones I undid.

My best friend looks at my boyfriend and he rushes to explain himself. "I was just getting ready."

"Or maybe...", she lets her words hang there and then turns toward me. I had walked up behind Oliver and she said,"I'm so excited for you", and then she pulled me into a fierce hug. She hugs me tightly and then gestures at what I'm wearing,"I love this outfit."

"Oliver bought it", I say quickly.

"Of course he did", his best friend says and then walks up to him. "Lover boy strikes again", Austin pats Oliver's cheek before going in to hug him. Oliver laughs and I pull my attention away from him, and down to my dress. It is a flowy long sleeve dress with a heart shaped neck. It is snitched at the waist but flows down to my tigh. Well as much as my thigh it covers. The dress is a few inches shy of my finger tip.

I look at Oliver and he looks at me, his eyes twinkling. I can see it, see the love he holds for me.

Oliver

I'm going to propose to her tonight.

I've been planning this ever since school started up again this year. I've held the title as her boyfriend for close to four years and I want to change it to fiance. God, I've been super nervous for this ever since we stepped foot in this country. But she has been making it harder, touching me, kissing me, and making it hard for me to hold in my thoughts.

This is easily the only secret I've been keeping from her and it has been getting harder to hold it in. Aurora has made it her mission to stall it, it seems. Her suggestive comments— actions have been getting me extra nervous.

Now, I sit beside her at the dinner table I prepared for this. I had lit a few candles at center of the table and even arranged a few bouquets. I wanted to make it good for my family and friends, I told her. She looks effortlessly pretty under the dim flourcent lights, her blonde hair flowing behind her hair. And the dress, God, I loved the dress when I bought it. But I love it even more on her. She knows how to make a dress look good.

"So", I start my hands getting clammy. I release it from hers and look at my parents. Both of them are offering me encouraging smiles while my mom is beaming. Austin and his girlfriend, Jude, are also looking at me.

This is my moment to make her officially mine. "Aurora."

"Amore?", she replies back and I stand up from my chair. I walk behind hers and say,"Do you want to..." This wasn't part of the plan. God, what had been the plan? Aurora stands up from her seat and places a hand on my face. I exhale at her touch and look at her, she looks worried.

"Are you okay?", she asks and I nod. I look at my mom and then back at my girlfriend.

"I'm going to get something from the kitchen, I'll be back", I say. She leans up and places a gentle kiss on my cheek. I beam at her and then turn on my heel and walk toward the kitchen. Once I get there, I place my hand in my pant pocket. I take out the ring box and place it in the palm of my hand. After a few minutes, I am ready to execute my plans.

I head back to the dining room and with encouraging looks from my parents and my bestfriend, I kneel down beside her chair.

"Aurora Moreno", I start, she looks back at me, her blonde hair flying sofity. Her eyes widen when she sees me on my knees and she immediately stands up. She walks beside me and I feel my heartbeat pick up. "I've known you for four years now. And for four years I have loved you. Spending time with you has been easily my favorite thing. Which is why it was so hard for me when we took a 'break'."

I hope my voice isn't wavering. "Aurora, I've seen you at your worst and yet you've always been strong. So freaking strong. I've had the privilage of watching you become stronger, if that's even possible. You might think that I saved you, but in reality you saved me. You've turned me into this young man who is worthy of loving you."

Her eyes wider and she lets out a soft sob. I find that her hand is shaking and that makes my hand shake harder as well. God, this is hard.

"I love you, la mia principessa. Will you do me the honor of marrying me?"

Her sob is louder than the answer she gives. She extends her hand at me and I place a soft hand on her wrist. I place the dainty ring onto her slender finger and once it's on, I waste no time standing up and pulling her into my arms.

Aurora and I were forever, I knew that in the way I knew that the earth revolved around the sun. I knew that we would always be together and even if we started to drift apart, there was going to be a stronger force working toward keeping us together.

I would love Aurora forever and I knew that, wrapped in her arms, that she would love me forever too. The both of us were stronger together; our love for each other was stronger together.

Our love was just beginning and I knew that it would only continue to blossom, never to wither away.

THE END